Happy Reading!

23-4-13

About the author

I was born in May 1981 in Suffolk and currently live in Hertfordshire. I have a Diploma in Administrative & Secretarial Procedures and work as the CEO's Personal Assistant at England's leading tyre distributor.

Aside from writing, my other passion in life is dance. I belong to a local group and participate in festivals throughout the country.

I know I am a writer because I wake each day knowing I must write. The magical effect of stringing words into one sequence or another never ceases to thrill me.

Any literary success of mine will be thanks to a constant desire to write and my family's support.

BENEATH THE DAISIES

DEDICATION

For Albert Beldon
1936 – 2009

"I may stumble, but I never fall!"

Jayne-Marie Barker

BENEATH THE DAISIES

AUSTIN & MACAULEY

A CIP catalogue record for this title is available from the British Library.

ISBN 978 1 84963 073 3

www.austinmacauley.com

First Published (2011)
Austin & Macauley Publishers Ltd.
25 Canada Square
Canary Wharf
London
E14 5LB

Printed & Bound in Great Britain

ACKNOWLEDGEMENTS

Thank you to my family, they make up my world and I never wish to be without them. Special thanks to my dad for helping me take the first step!

I wish to thank Dennis Barker for his valuable career advice over the years of my apprenticeship!

A special thank you to Alex Evans and everybody at Pixmoor Junior School in Letchworth Garden City for affording me their time, and showing me what life as a primary school teacher is really like!

Thank you to Chris Brabrook and Vikki Dugid-Newell who were both so helpful to me during my research – if there are any inaccuracies I assure you they're my mistakes and not theirs!

An extra special thanks to my friend Charlotte Dixon for all her help proofreading!

Prologue

The rain was heavy, pelting down in sheets, droplets the size of hail stones thumping at the windowpanes. The early November wind growled vociferously like a predator at large. The clock struck ten, its chime resonating through her heart like a drum. Katie Bass had just heard the headlines of the evening news. Her husband was listening to it on the wireless. Slightly shaking and feeling peculiar she had mounted the stairs of their semi-detached house, and now stood in the back bedroom by the window. She stood alone, in the dark.

The black starless night loomed in at her menacingly through the single plate glass window. The moon was whole, bold, a shine of mist coating it protectively. She eyed it sceptically as it shimmered over the gardens like a spotlight, particles of dust suspended in the air like trapped ice. A dart of movement made her flinch. A cat probably, or a squirrel, she told herself sternly. She took a deep breath and closed her eyes. No, no, no, a silent scream.

Katie looked around her room, anything to take her mind elsewhere. It was fairly small, neat, lined with shelves and storage cupboards and in keeping with the latest minimalist style. The clutter of the previous century was now considered "Victorian" and Katie, like most housewives, strived to maintain her home to the best of her ability within the confines of argument the housekeeper afforded her. The income from her husband's family business in America had dwindled each year; she had struggled to maintain the standards of living they had set out with. Regrettably they were now down to a staff of

13

three but they managed. At least she and her husband were deeply happy, until today. Katie had a horrible feeling that things were never going to be the same again. Now she couldn't imagine being happy ever again.

It was as if the afternoon's events had clouded her life forever. All she saw when she closed her eyes was the sharp knife, the blade sinking in. The clarity of it was excruciatingly real. Everything else was misty as if she were looking through a tight-knit fog. There was no way out of it. The afternoon had suffocated her, strangled every flake of hope until she stood, beyond all help, her faith in human kind desecrated.

Katie contemplated taking out her embroidery but her body felt fidgety and her mind disturbed. Her arms still throbbed violently each time she moved. The encounter had cost her weak limbs a high price. Fortunately it had been the staffs afternoon off; her housekeeper had been out taking tea with her sister and the two parlour maids had gone to the flicks with their gentleman friends. Perhaps it would have been easier if they had all been home, they too would have heard the petrifying screams.

The images flicked through her mind defiantly, like a stuck ticker tape. She tired to blot the atrocious pictures out, closing her eyes and squinting tight. It was no use; her eyelids could not shield the view. She wondered just how long she would have to suffer this for.

Katie went to the window, her footsteps padding silently across the threadbare beige carpet. The solid curtain of rain was coming down in stair rods and the wind was growing stronger, gathering its strength with each whip of annihilation. The newly planted conifer trees at the end of next door's garden were fatalities of the wind, propelled around savagely. The canes didn't look half strong enough to hold them steady. She wondered about ringing Frederick to tell him, but then decided not to. It wasn't a good enough excuse to ring anyway. She had racked her brains for a decent excuse to ring up since four o'clock but nothing solid had come her way. There was nothing she could do to help him now. It was all much too late, far too late.

Katie watched the baby trees dancing in the winds; were their short lives to end already? It wasn't the first she had witnessed today. Her arms did hurt. She flinched as she moved them, wrapping them around herself so she resembled a strait jacket. Entrapped into her situation, silenced and under someone else's control. Yes, a strait jacket demonstrated it perfectly. Prisons didn't always have to have walls and bars in order to exist.

Frederick's back door slapped back against the brickwork. She jumped, heard it snap like a broken bone, and cast her gaze out over her neighbour's garden. Out came Frederick, a large bundle in his arms...a bundle wrapped in a thick brown cloth. The kind of cloth used in packing trunks at the turn of the century.

Katie held her breath as he rested the bundle carefully on the ground. It fell limp as he relinquished his hold. It was long, a lone foot exposed to the elements at one end. Katie's breath caught in her throat. She had expected the sirens of the ambulance or the police, waited for them, watched for them in case they had arrived in silence, it being clearly too late to save the innocent lives, but when they hadn't come she had wondered even more. She had no idea what Frederick would do, but she had never expected this drastic action. Surely he wasn't just going to... no, no, he couldn't!

Katie squinted through the storm, her view distorted by the relentless rain. Her head began to ache. She felt her pulse quicken with the anxiety. The brightness of the glistening red sandal on the elegant woman's foot spoke out to her in the dark wet night. It was cold. She shivered. She closed her eyes and opened them again; the motion nightmare was still there, right in front of her. The heating hadn't kicked into life yet. She wrapped her arms around herself even tighter. Her body temperature dropped suddenly, whether it was from the sight or the coolness in the room she couldn't be certain. The shoe flashed an unpleasant memory across her mind. She trembled fiercely, felt the goose pimples on her arms and her heart almost stop with fright.

Where was Clarissa? Where were the housekeeper and the cook? Surely they had returned by now…Katie closed her eyes and inhaled deeply. When she opened them again Frederick had vanished. He was stomping back towards the house. She could almost hear the slushy noise as his heavy waterproof boot-clad feet splashed into the muddy grass. He wasn't going to leave the woman there, alone, lying helplessly on the lawn, was he? A cold sweat crept over Katie's palms and her stomach lurched over in protest. She took a deep breath, resisting the urge to vomit. She hadn't had an appetite and had picked at her evening meal. Albert had noticed of course but so far she had managed to get away with 'I'm not feeling too well, I'll be all right in the morning.' That wasn't going to wash once dawn broke.

Frederick marched back out of the house next door, his footsteps squelching down the lawn with another bundle. This time much larger, he was struggling under the weight of it, the clothed bundle much bulkier than the first. With a thud Katie could only imagine the bundle was put down next to the woman with the red sandal. The second bundle was handled with considerably less care. No surprise really, she thought.

Katie realised she was still holding her breath, her hands clasped together as if in prayer. It would be decent after all, to say a few words. She watched in horror as Frederick vanished again, into the shed at the base of the garden, seconds later returning with a large shovel.

Frederick's muscles worked quickly, the silver spade reflecting the moon's rays as he thrust it into the ground, his heel sinking it still further deep. She watched his muscles flexing unceasingly with the exertion. She watched him launch the soil up in the air, over his shoulder. The mountain of mud behind him grew steadily. Over an hour later she still stood there, watching intently.

'Katie?' it was Albert. He crept up behind her so softly, her concentration solely on Frederick. Her silhouette spread out on the carpet before her husband's feet, captured by the light from the now open door onto the landing.

'Bert!' she was startled, attempted to move towards him, away from the window. It was for his own protection he didn't see Frederick's labours. He could testify to nothing then, nothing at all. Complete innocent. She envied him that much, and that alone. 'Bert, no!' she cried as he headed towards the window. His gasp was loud and raspy. His mouth was left in a perfect O shape, the impression stuck on his face like a mask. 'Bert,' she said again, a softer voice, coming up beside him and watching as Frederick began to lift the larger bulkier bundle up.

'Oh my God!' Bert said, 'are they...' Katie nodded her head in silent respect as the pair of them watched Frederick placing the body in the hole. Albert pulled Katie closer to him, his arms wrapped around her waist. She clung to him. Much better than the strait jacket, still she knew her prison walls were never coming down. The nightmare would never end.

The rain was filling Fredericks hole like a determined lake, the muddy rainwater oozing out from the mountain behind him. He worked hastily, placing the smaller body, the woman, in the hole as well. Feverishly he piled the sloppy wet mud back into the hole, the rain overflowing the grave as he fought hard against the elements. Just twenty minutes later Frederick was levelling the ground. He returned the mucky shovel to the shed and stood on the lawn by the fresh grave.

For the first time he looked up towards their window. They stood still, their eyes locking into Frederick. Katie could see the water dripping down Frederick's face like a wall of tears. His grief cloaked him, his body oblivious to the near freezing temperature and the angry howl of wind that threatened destruction with a single swipe. It was over now.

Whether or not he saw them they couldn't say, but any movement would certainly have given them away. Katie held her breath, her chest heaved inwards with the fear of moving even the slightest bit. Frederick looked down at the ground, the rain still pouring down his face like a fountain. After a couple of minutes of staring at the muddy lawn Frederick turned, his head hung low, and walked back towards the house, the door slamming behind him.

17

Chapter One

March 2009

Sophie was busy unpacking a box of utensils, saucepans and plates in the kitchen when the front door bell rang. It would be Mr Taylor, she thought, well his timing was good. She lowered her armful back into the box with a minor clatter, rubbed her hands on her jean-clad thighs and padded softly towards the front door in her stripy socks.

The sky looked momentarily devoid of sunshine but the blueness was breaking through in large patches. An unexpected burst of sunshine flashed into her eyes as she swung the door open and her breath caught in her throat as she looked at him for the first time. He starred back at her with eyes the colour of stardust.

Andrew Taylor smiled at his new client, a broad smile that made his eyes sparkle and her knees wane. So it wasn't a cliché; she thought fleetingly, this type of instant infusion of emotions did exist. A moment passed and neither said a word. The smiles extended, dangerously heading towards a full minute before he spoke.

'Miss Harris?' his voice was thick and soft like golden syrup. She found herself lost for words.

'Y...yes,' she whispered.

'Andrew Taylor,' he offered, extending his hand, 'you can call me Andy.'

'Sophie.' The warmth of his fingers around hers was making her mind fuzzy.

'Where do you want me to start Sophie?' he asked, his blue eyes smiling at her. Hearing him say her name distracted her again. *Get a grip* she told herself. His hand was still in hers, the crimson shade filling her as she released him.

'Um, um, the garden,' she said without thinking. Of course it would be better to start with the decorating but it was too late now.

'Right, ok, shall I go around the side with the tools?' he offered, indicating the gate to his left that led to the back garden.

'Yes please,' she said, 'I'll meet you in the garden.' She shut the door with gusto; leant heavily against it and realised she had been holding her breath. *Pull yourself together Sophie* she chastised herself. *Just pull yourself together.*

Quickly she ran to the back door, pulled on some shoes and hopped out into the garden. Andy was unloading an array of gardening tools into the middle of the lawn. The sun was reflecting off his tanned arms creating a shine. He looked like a god and she felt suddenly weak again. Twitchingly she fiddled with the knot at the nape of her open white blouse over the flimsy cami top beneath.

'What would you like doing out here then?' he asked, sensing her arrival and unwittingly slicing into her daydream.

'Um, would you like some tea?' she offered, smiling and hoping for an affirmative to allow herself some time alone. Clearly the first lecture she had paid herself had already fallen by the wayside.

'Yeah, that'd be nice, thanks,' he flashed her another wide smile from his stance bent over the tools on the lawn. 'Shall I get started?' She nodded at him in silence. 'Where?'

'I was hoping for a pond,' she told him, the words tumbling out hurriedly, 'about here,' she pointed to the lawn.

'Right ok, well I'll start on that then.'

'Thanks. I'll just go, and, go and make the tea,' she breathed and skipped back into the house. The day was unusually warm for the time of year, or was it just her? She couldn't decide which. Her eyes flicked to him through the kitchen window like a magnet.

Sophie clicked on the kettle, took out two mugs and dropped Tetley tea bags into them absent-mindedly. She was being ridiculous, silly, it was just a moment. It would pass. She would probably go back out there with the mugs of tea and wonder what all the fuss was about. Yes, she would be fine, just fine. Convinced by her own assertions she poured the hot water over the tea bags. It was time to face the music.

'Do you actually know what you're doing?' she asked as she bought the mugs of tea out into the back garden. Andy was beginning to break out into a labour induced sweat. Beads of sweat along his arms glistened in the light. A sizeable hole was already underway.

'Of course,' Andy smiled, 'I'm a professional, remember?' he laughed, his blue eyes sparkling at her with interest.

'Sorry, yes of course you are, I didn't mean to, er, to...' She could feel the scarlet shade rising from somewhere in the pit of her stomach. With alarming rapidity it reached her face and spread out like a flame.

'Hey, I was joking, relax!' Andy took a large gulp of his tea and rested the mug down on an upturned recycling crate that had previously housed his tools. Sophie drank quickly, almost burning the top of her mouth and trying desperately not to look at Andy's tanned biceps flexing with the strain. 'How big do you want this to be then?' he asked her, grabbing the shovel again.

As big as you like... she blushed to herself. *Get a grip.*

'About to here,' she gestured, pointing her toes. Her heart felt as if it had leapt into her mouth. He sank the shovel back into the soft earth. Sophie watched the sun dance off his dark blond hair with interest, her pulse quickening. She felt oddly faint. A frenzied numbness took over her legs.

'I tell you, it's getting smaller the more I have to dig!' he reached for his tea and paused, the shovel dug upright into the hole in the ground. 'Thanks,' he said, indicating the now empty purple mug. Sophie flashed a smile at him, wiped a stray strand of her chocolate brown hair aside and hopped nervously onto the other foot. Unsure what to say next, she looked up at the sun and followed a bird flying across the roof, shielding her eyes with her arm, anything to keep from staring at the most gorgeous man she had ever seen.

Why did he have to be so fabulous? It wasn't fair. Moments before he had arrived she hadn't noticed the thread bare material in her blouse, or the fact that her jeans were faded and torn at the knees. She was dressed for unpacking dusty boxes, painting walls, heaving furniture around the lounge, certainly not fit for what could turn out to be the most important first impression of her life.

'So,' he said, tunnelling into her dreams again, 'when did you move in?'

'Is it that obvious?' she asked, surprised.

'Well, you have boxes in the window,' he smiled at her. 'You get used to the signs in my line of work,' he mused. 'Nice road this, hope you'll be happy here.'

'Thank you.'

'I've done a fair bit of work in this area, nice people.' He continued to dig as he spoke, deep effortless-looking plunges into the earth. Sophie glanced at the growing hole, the soft earth crumbling at his command.

'Oh good, always nice to know,' she said, mesmerised by the speed with which he progressed deep into the ground.

'Recently then?'

'Just yesterday,' she whispered, 'my grandmother died and she left the house to me.' Her own voice sounded distant to her, oddly quiet. It was as if someone were playing it back to her from a recording riddled with echoes.

'Oh, I'm sorry,' he looked at her, their eyes locking in a heartbeat.

'It's alright, she had a great life.' Sophie's hair bounced with her affirmative nod.

Silence prevailed for about thirty seconds. Worry lines creased Sophie's brow; she hadn't meant to tell him – a perfect stranger – about her grandmother's death. Even though he was quite literally a perfect stranger.

'Wow, you didn't waste much time in calling me out, not that I'm complaining you understand,' he smiled again. His teeth were really white she thought, and his mouth was so inviting. She mentally pulled herself together.

'Well I wanted to er, to get things moving,' she stammered, 'you know, so much to do, so little time and all… can I help you at all?'

'Probably not,' he said honestly, 'besides, you've hired me to do it so no point in your getting all mucky too.' Andy threw the shovel down into the earth again, a loud clink stunting his efforts. 'You've got buried treasure,' he said with a laugh, straightening himself and leaping down into the hole to investigate.

Sophie picked up the two mugs and contemplated going back inside. She felt magnetically drawn to him but there was only so much she could think of to say, besides what she wanted to ask him like *are you married? Have you got any children? Do you love me? Oh my God, you've got the most beautiful body, any chance you want to spend the rest of your life with me?*

From somewhere another clink of the shovel roused her attention. She watched the colour drain from Andy's face in an instant. He seemed transfixed by the hole in the ground. 'What?' she half yelled. 'What are you glaring at…' the mugs fell from her hands and crashed to the ground as she stepped towards the hole. No…no…it couldn't be…

Andy looked at her, resting the shovel down on the undisturbed lawn and came towards her side. She held onto him tightly as if it might leap up and attack them. Suddenly it didn't matter that they were relative strangers. It was just necessary to feel the living…Andy wrapped her into his arms and gently but firmly turned her to face away from the hole.

'It can't be…' His eyes moved from her face to the hole, back to her face and then, slowly, he let her alone and moved towards the hole. 'Don't look,' he warned.

'No, don't touch it!' she cried. A cool breeze snaked its way through the garden. The sun slid dubiously behind a cloud as if in hiding. Sophie tugged on Andy's shirt. 'Leave it. Just cover it all up and I'll ring the police, please!' she begged. 'Leave it alone. If it's what we think it is we can't touch it.' Andy moved back towards her side. He hugged her quickly and gave her a gentle shove back towards the house.

'Go put something stronger in these,' he commanded, proffering the empty mugs from the grass. She ran towards the back door into the kitchen, in search of whisky.

As she watched Andy shovel the soil back into the hole she dialled the local police station. Her fingers felt frozen but on the third attempt she managed the correct number and listened impatiently to the dialling tone.

'Hello, Suffolk Police, how can I help you?' a kind voice answered.

'I think...I think...' her breath wouldn't come easily. She could feel herself hyperventilating.

'Just calm down Miss, breathe slowly and tell me clearly what seems to be the matter.' The operator's voice was cool and collected. Sophie inhaled deeply and closed her eyes.

'Well...we were just digging in the garden...and...we saw a bone, I thought it might have been a dog's bone or something...but...then we saw a skull. I think it's a human skull! I'm not sure what to do!' her voice rose steadily.

'Take a deep breath Miss,' the operator said. 'Slow down. Tell me slowly...'

'There's a dead body buried in my garden!' she wailed, beginning to lose control all too quickly. 'Can you please...'

Outside Andy was still shovelling the dirt back into the hole, covering their buried friend. Sophie twisted to see him through the window, the telephone cord curling around her fingers and cutting the circulation.

'I'll send an officer around immediately,' the kind voice told her down the line. 'Don't worry now. Can you tell me your address?' Another deep breath and Sophie relayed the details.

Outside Andy was starring down at the grass, disbelief spread over his face, his shovel abandoned at his feet.

From the quietness of the kitchen Sophie looked out over her garden. Her father would be furious if he knew. She debated telling him but didn't feel up to it. It would wait, the bones weren't going anywhere by the looks of things.

Sophie's hands shook as the dark brown liquid slopped into glasses noisily. Andy took the bottle from her and replaced the cap and pulled out a chair for her. She followed his lead and fell heavily into the wooden kitchen chair, rested her head on her hands and took a deep breath. A companionable silence surrounded them like a blanket.

Andy moved to the kitchen sink to wash his hands and sat down at the table in silence, looking around the kitchen. The oven, hob and extraction hood were so well hidden he had to look twice just to locate them. There wasn't even any point in guessing where the fridge and freezer hid. A large white butler sink occupied the work surface beneath the window overlooking the garden. He shoved the box of utensils slightly away and shifted his chair closer towards her.

'Are you all right?' his voice was soft and despite the shock of the find she found herself managing to flash a half smile at him.

'Yes I think so,' she said, gesturing towards the whisky and taking a large sip of her own. 'Are you?'

'Yeah, you don't have to worry about me, you'd be surprised at the things people bury in their gardens,' he attempted a half-hearted chuckle and rather unconvincingly drained his glass in one. So it had shaken him she thought, but he was far from admitting as much to her.

'Really, like what?' she asked, feeling better already. 'Don't tell me this isn't the first set of human remains you've unearthed?'

As if it knew the sun was masked by a thick cloud and a shadow quickly spread over their cosy encounter at the kitchen table. Sophie finished her whisky and re-filled both their glasses. It was purely shock she told herself, not usually being a big drinker at all, let alone strong whisky in the middle of the day.

'No, not quite, but people do odd things. Come across a fair few pets in my time, quite a few things people just wanted to get rid of. This isn't the first time police have been called, so don't worry I know the drill. They'll turn up, put up one of those white tents most probably, and gather it all up in plastic

24

bags. That'll be it for today, you can relax, we've done all we can for now. They'll probably ban you from entering the garden for a while, nothing drastic though.'

Sophie sighed heavily.

'Yes, I expect you're right,' she said finally. 'Still, it's horrible. This house has been in my family for decades. Chances are those skeletons are...'

'Ssh...Don't say it,' he interrupted her, covering her mouth with his hand. 'You don't know that. Shall we talk about something else?' His body warmth made her feel giddy. She nodded her head in agreement as he retrieved his hand. What was wrong with her, why, even after the horrible find, did she still want to rip the clothes off this gorgeous man who sat inches away from her at the kitchen table?

'Why don't you tell me about yourself,' she asked, 'distract me,' she breathed, resting her chin on her hands. The whisky was quite strong. Andy took another gulp and leant forward towards her. Sophie felt his warm breath on her face, his lips inches from hers, and suddenly the skeletons were forgotten, at least temporarily.

'All right, what do you want to know?' he asked her, his eyes searching hers and finding only intrigued mystery.

'Everything,' she whispered.

'Ok, where to start,' he mused, 'when I left school I worked for Lloyds Nursery. They had a gardening team, you know like you hire them out, like you've hired me. A bit like groundforce but without Alan Titchmarsh,' he beamed. She smiled encouragingly.

'Anyway, one day I was asked to help with some planting,' he continued. 'It was good and I thought I'd like to give it a shot. It was better than heaving around the ornaments and bags of fertiliser all day. So when a vacancy came up for an apprenticeship I applied and they gave it to me.' Andy smiled at her, paused.

'Go on,' she urged.

'It was a two year course. I worked for them for a while after I finished the course and I was sent out with some of the other guys on jobs. It was fun most of the time, hard work but a good laugh. 'bout six months back a friend of the family asked if I'd do a private job for him. Paid really well. Didn't think much about it until the week after. He'd recommended me to this guy he worked with and I got another private job. It sort of sprung off quickly and I thought I'd give it a go at going full time on my own. Bit scary at first mind,' he smiled at her again. 'Didn't know if I was being a complete idiot but so far so good. I left Lloyds couple of months ago and I've been run off my feet with work ever since.'

'Sounds like you know what you want,' her voice was quiet, even quieter than she realised. His eyes sparkled at her.

'I always know what I want,' he told her, 'and I usually get it,' he promised, the static growing.

'You don't say,' she teased and he smiled brightly. 'You must be very successful' she murmured.

'I don't know if it'll last but at the moment things are good.'

'What about in the winter?' she quizzed. His eyes were so close to hers now she could barely drag her gaze away.

'There'll be consultation work,' he said quietly. 'And I've done the first term of interior decoration at college so hopefully I'll get more decorating and handy jobs in the colder months.'

'Um,' Sophie hummed, 'sounds like a good plan to me.'

'Hope so,' he said.

'What happens next?' she asked

'In reality or in a perfect world?' he teased her. She giggled lightly.

'In reality,' she whispered with reluctance. 'We'll come to the perfect world later,' she promised with a smile. 'What will you do if the business takes off, will you take on extra staff?'

'Yeah, I think so,' he breathed, the warmth merging with her own, 'I'm already trying to expand, sow the seeds as it were. I've taken on Bill as an assistant. He's retired really, he's 64, so he comes cheap,' he chuckled, 'although he knows the score so I don't need to spend much time training him.'

'I see,' she whispered.

'When he finally retires for good I'll get a full timer I think, younger chap, school leaver maybe. Someone I can...' he thought for a minute for the right word '...mould.'

'Mould hey?'

'Yeah, I like things to be just so,' he teased her, his finger tips tracing her arm. A tingling sprinted through her body. 'There's a new contract out for tender and I'm going for that too,' he continued.

'Ambitious,' she agreed, 'that's always a good sign,' she whispered.

'Really, I'm glad to hear it,' his fingertips created little circles on her arm, their warmth heating her from within. 'It'll be hard work if I get it but, you know, be worth it in the end. Some things are worth working for.' His smile would have floored her if she were standing, as it was she felt her whole being melt at will.

'Shall I show you around the house?' she offered, almost not wanting to move. 'We could look at the decorating first instead.' Her voice was barely audible.

'That's a good idea,' he agreed, leaning further towards her. 'Do you want *every* room decorated?'

Sophie nodded slowly.

'Absolutely every room, it'll take you a while I imagine,' she said quietly.

'I'm not in a rush,' he smiled at her. His lips were half a breath away from hers when the doorbell chimed and they sprang apart like fire-crackers.

'Oh,' Sophie said, her face flushed pink, 'that must be the p... sorry,' she stammered, 'I'd better get the door.'

Andy sat back in his chair, watched her beautiful frame walk from the kitchen door into the open hallway past the staircase and towards the front door. He downed the rest of his whisky and smiled. Despite the unfortunate find in the garden he had a good feeling about this particular job.

'It's this way,' Sophie led the policeman and his crew through the house into the garden. Andy got up from the table and began to wash the whisky glasses in the sink. The police

27

were in the garden for quite some time, digging up the same spot and asking Sophie questions. She stood on the basic patio area, the conservatory to her left, spanning the width of the living room. Andy looked at the perfect line of her back. Behind her were the kitchen window and the back door in the middle of the house, almost in line with the front. Andy saw her gesture for him to come out and exited the house via the back door.

'So Sir, you were digging here,' Sergeant Wells pointed to the spot where his colleagues were carefully selecting the bones. He was a short and fairly plump man with a pink round face and mousy hair that curled at his ears. His uniform was crisp, the silver buckles glinting in the sunlight. Sophie turned away and Andy reached for her hand, drew her into his embrace.

'Yes,' he said over Sophie's shoulder. 'I got that far and then we covered it back over and rang you.' He shielded his eyes from the sun with his free hand.

'Ok, there's not much else we can ask at this time. We'll be as quick as we can. We'll be treating this garden as a crime scene Miss Harris,' Sergeant Wells told her. 'We'll need to tape it off so no-one can contaminate the area. I'm sorry but you'll have to stay out the garden for the time being.'

'That's alright officer,' Sophie stammered. 'I don't think I want to go into the garden for a while.' Andy had been right, she thought, clever as well as handsome. There had to be catch...

'Our SOC lads are just taking any DNA testing and prints they can. We're waiting for the doctor then we can move them,' Sergeant Wells indicated the hole with a nod. A team of five were erecting a white tent over the hole and ushered them further out the way. He pushed her gently towards the house, his hand on the small of her back. Andy took his lead and pulled Sophie closer towards him.

'The doctor?' she queried.

'I know it seems strange Miss but we have to have the doctor confirm that life is extinct before we can move them. He should be along in a minute.'

'Sir!' one of the white-coated men produced a red shoe out the ground like a flag. They huddled together like children in a playground. Sophie clung to Andy, trying not to watch.

'Excuse me,' Sergeant Wells mumbled and sprinted the couple of feet towards the almost erected tent. A ladies red shoe and a torn silk neck scarf, both covered in mud. Sophie shivered and Andy held her tighter.

'Them?' she whispered into Andy's shoulder. 'Did he say them, as in more than one?

The officer returned, the shoe and scarf in hand. His shadow cast out behind him like a cloak over the horrid scene.

'Do you recognise these Miss?'

'No, I'm sorry,' Sophie said quietly. 'I've never seen them before.'

'Ok, you can take the young lady back inside if you like Sir,' Wells told Andy with a half nod before turning back towards his team.

'Thank you,' Andy said, leading Sophie back into the house.

'Let's get this show on the road,' they heard the officer calling. 'Where's the damn doctor? And who is our MCS?'

'I am of course, son,' a new voice ventured, 'who did you expect?' A tall thin inspector with a cigarette in his mouth and a brown checked hat turned the corner from the gate, just as Sophie and Andy opened the back door in order to escape into to the sanity of the house.

'Hello,' the inspector smiled at them, lifting his hat briefly. 'Good morning, fine day isn't it? I'm inspector Allen,' he extended his hand. She took it limply. 'So, has the Sergeant taken down your particulars?'

'Yes inspector,' Sophie told him.

'Righto,' he beamed. 'I'll have a word,' he informed her, his fingers toying his grey moustache as he waltzed towards his sergeant, a few giant strides away.

Sophie now stood at the kitchen window watching. People of various sizes and shapes covered in white paper-looking suits marched about the garden. Little plastic bags and what looked to Sophie like a pastry brush were being passed around

29

like a children's party game. Did it really need to take this long? They were very studious with their facemasks and plastic gloves. She would be hard pushed to distinguish between the men and the women, they all looked identical. Alien almost. One of them stomped around with a clipboard marking down silent acknowledgements from various colleagues. The uniformed officers stood guard around the edges to the gate and to the front of the house. Eventually a man in a grey woollen overcoat arrived carrying a black leather doctors' bag. He stood over the hole and glanced quickly into it. He spoke briefly to the inspector and sauntered off again.

The house stood proud and tall, a brick semi built in the nineteenth century, its chimney rising up into the blue tinted sky. Her family had occupied the house for years. The driveway was gravelled and took over most of what would once have been a front garden.

The hallway ran from the front door to the kitchen. The staircase ran up the right hand side and beneath that an alcove that Sophie remembered once having shelves in when her grandmother had been alive. The shelves must have been removed since she had last visited. Sophie led Andy up the stairs, the handrail was flaking; white specks of paint falling like confetti.

'Shall we...' Sophie indicated the stairs. 'I want to do something. I can't just sit here idly.'

'Of course,' he said. 'We'd better see to that hadn't we?' Andy said, indicating the handrail, his fingers brushing alongside hers. Tingles filtered through her like champagne bubbles and she felt slightly flushed.

'Yes I guess so,' she agreed. 'Thank you,' she said.

'For what?' he looked surprised as they came to pause on the bottom few steps. Sophie looked into his eyes, the moments stretched out like a motion picture.

'Trying to look after me, to distract me, for not running away,' she said. He afforded her another one of his winning smiles as she led the way up the stairs.

The bathroom was opposite the top of the staircase. It was decorated in old Victorian black and white tiles; similar effect to those used in the kitchen and clearly needed no work whatsoever.

The ceiling in the smallest of the four bedrooms was white, a small flake storm brewing but nothing a spot of paint couldn't fix. Decorative moulding of the ceiling had developed into a work of art. An entire ring of angels and cat-like creatures fluttered around the tops of the walls.

'Can you fix that?' she enquired and he nodded at her. 'Give some thought to the colours in these rooms so we can purchase them in bulk supply. It'll save a lot of money.' She smiled at him and avoided the view from the window where the erected white tent was already covering a good half of her lawn.

Andy moved her on, his hands on her waist. The next two rooms stood empty with small windows, bare bulbs dangling limply and shadows stained into the walls.

'Some very clever lighting must have controlled the mood in these rooms,' Sophie mused. The lamps had long since vanished, leaving only their grubby ghost marks on the walls. Some of the plaster around the holes was visible. Andy ran a finger over it and rubbed his hand on his trousers leg.

'Yes, well I can help you choose lights if you like.' Andy told her. 'These are fine, nothing to worry about,' he said.

'They were taken out,' she explained. 'We thought the house would have to be sold to pay for nursing care but then she…' Andy nodded. 'It wasn't expected quite so soon.'

'Don't worry, it'll get better than this, give it time,' Andy soothed, taking her hand again and leading her into the last room, the master bedroom, which overlooked the front of the house. A large room greeted them. Sophie's double bed was covered in an inviting pastel pink duvet. A large wooden wardrobe stood to the side wall and dressing table by the window. Suitcases of unpacked clothes lined the floor. The room had a pretty bay window with a seat. 'So just easy painting up here then,' he summarised stepping over the suitcases and looking a her, 'unless you'd prefer wallpaper?'

'No, I hate wallpaper,' she shook her head most vigorously. Andy chuckled. 'Paint will be fine. We'll pick out colours as soon as possible,' she affirmed with another nod.

'Nice curtains,' he commented sarcastically.

'Very droll,' she quipped looking at her temporary bed sheets that acted as curtains for her first night in the new house. 'Another thing I need to get around to today.' They looked out the window at the police loading bags into the boot of the car. It sat on the street like a beacon. 'I sure have made an entrance in the street haven't I!' she said sadly. Andy squeezed her hand.

'Don't worry about it. We'd better go downstairs,' he said reluctantly, 'in case the police need to get going. Looks like they've almost finished out there.' She nodded slowly. 'You can show me the lounge,' he smiled at her as she descended the stairs.

'That's the largest room,' she said, 'do you think we should start there?'

'If you like, it's up to you.'

To the left of the front door and base of the staircase was the lounge. It was a large room, stretching from the front bay window, again with a seat, back towards the French doors where the house originally stopped. The French doors looked old, their frames in need of a new varnish. Beyond the doors was the conservatory that presently sat empty, its large waist height glass panels and ceiling in dire need of a wash and polish. Sophie inspected it spanning from the far wall adjoining the neighbour's house to the edge of the living room; it was certainly impressive.

Pieces of furniture sat in the middle of the room like oddments. The carpet was dark and covered the entire room and the hallway blending up the staircase to the landing above. Around the window seat in the bay at the front of the house some cushions had been left over by the clearance men. Sophie took a seat in the window and looked out into the gravel driveway where her car sat contentedly.

'Er, Miss,' the police sergeant's voice carried loudly from the hallway.

'Yes,' she said, popping out into the hallway and feeling much better. The whisky must have kicked in.

'I've some bad news for you I'm afraid.'

'Other than the human remains in my garden?' her eyebrows arched in mock surprise. 'Surprise me, don't tell me you've found some other grisly thing out there?'

'Not quite Miss, but I have to tell you it looks like the remains of two people, not one. A male and a female we think but we'll know more once our lab has had a chance to go over the remains.'

Sophie felt faint and made a move for the bottom stair.

'It'll be a few days Miss but we'll get back to you soon as we can. In the meantime, please try not to go into the garden, just in case we need to dig over anymore'. Sophie nodded at him wordlessly; it was the last place she wanted to go. Dig some more! Did they think it was a mass grave or something?

'We'll be calling on a forensic archaeologist for this one I reckon,' the sergeant assured her boldly. 'I wouldn't be surprised if they pulled out all the stops.'

'Why?' Andy asked

'Well the shoe and the scarf we found date back to the twenties or early thirties. Looks like whoever they were, they've been there for quite a while,' he explained. 'There are a few other fragments of clothes we can go on too. Don't worry though, we'll be taking everything away with us now but please like I said, don't go into the garden.'

'Right, yes of course,' she managed to sigh. 'Thank you, sergeant.'

'Blimey, I'm dreading the paperwork I can tell you; just think how many missing persons they'll be dating all that damned way back!'

'Indeed,' Sophie said sarcastically. 'I expect you'll manage,' she sighed. Thick skinned she thought, straight over his head.

'Oh one last thing, Miss,' the officer spun back around, half way out the front door. 'You've no idea who they might be I suppose?'

ATWOOD CHRONICLE

Bodies Beneath The Lawn!

Skeletons have been unearthed from beneath the lawn of a local property. Local police have kept the new owner of the property out of the garden now for nearly a week.

The skeletons are said to have been buried at least fifty-five years previously, long before the current owner of the property was in residence.

The skeletons are yet to be identified as male or female but it is thought that one is most certainly a young male. At present police are treating the deaths as suspicious although suspects are a long way off, according to a local source who wished to remain anonymous. "The remains have yet to be attached to anybody registered as missing so the cause of death is not a priority at the moment, although it will obviously be investigated thoroughly in time. The first thing to do is establish who these people were!"

Spokeswoman for the local police constabulary, WPC Clarke, claims that the skeletons are of great importance to the understanding of local history. "When people go missing it is often their relatives or close friends who report their absence, but there are people out there without anybody who would miss them immediately, and that's where these sorts of finds can help. Often these individuals are reported missing when it is much too late for police to act in an effective way."

If you can help with the investigation in any way contact your local police station, good luck to our diligent police force. They certainly have their work cut out with this one!

Chapter Two

5th January 1935 – Diary of Elise Harris nee Trent

Today I feel empty. I am thinking about when I was four. These thoughts always do this to me and much as I try to push them away they are persistent. Today they win me over and I am beaten into submission once again.

It was 1899 and my parents abandoned me. I remember it being winter, a harsh winter, but I'm not sure what month it is, or even if it is before or after Christmas. It wasn't such a big event for me, Christmas, being orphaned. Well, kind of. I think about how cold I was, sitting alone on the freezing stone steps; the damp seeping into my cotton skirt and making my bottom feel numb like ice. It must have been the early hours as it was very dark. The stars were bright. I watched them twinkle; the dusky light orbiting them seemed comforting.

I heard the milkman's cart in the next street. It paused. Rattle rattle, clink, clink. The glass bottles rested on the steps and the cart moved on a couple of feet. Rattle rattle, clink, clink. Again, it moved. Only I stayed still.

'Easy boy,' I heard the milkman soothing his horse. The clip clop of the hooves echoed through the empty night sky and I curled up tighter on the step.

The air whipped around my face, its frosty temperature lapping at my cheeks like a torment. I wondered if the milkman would come my way. Would he see me? I was scared. I did not like strangers but I really wanted to see someone, a nice kind person who would give me a blanket, or perhaps take me inside where it was warm.

I couldn't read very well back then but I knew the sign outside the door said home. I thought that was nice. I remember thinking that perhaps I had moved home. I wondered why my mum and dad hadn't moved with me.

After what seemed like forever I felt very sleepy. I was too cold to fall asleep though. I curled up on the icy steps and sat up against the door. I had to wait. That was all they said to me before they left. Wait. Wait until morning and the door will be opened. Again I sat wondering why they hadn't moved with me.

I do not remember falling asleep but I must have dozed off for a time. The next thing I remember is the dawn. The sun crept up between the gaps in the houses. My view was suddenly burst from the centre outwards. The blinding light startled me. I rubbed my eyes. I was frightened. I sat wondering how much longer I had to wait before the door would be opened.

The birds were chirping loudly. From far off I could hear the steam whistle and the factory starting up for another routine day's offerings. There was dampness in the air, a clammy mist that clung stubbornly to my clothes.

I heard a sound. I think it was a bell. Then, from my left I spied a shape coming towards me. I rubbed my eyes again and shuffled about on the stone steps. I felt numb still, tingles toying with my body. I shook my legs and arms and stood up slowly. My leg was still asleep and pins and needles prickled me as I moved. I was still cold and the bricks had marked my face where I had leant against the wall.

The bell sounded again. The shape coming towards me began to be clearer. It was a man. He was riding a bicycle. He threw things, newspapers I think. The bell sounded again. He came closer, stopped his bike and stared at me.

'Here you go,' he said. In his outstretched hand was a newspaper. I walked gingerly towards him, my legs felt like jelly, and I took the paper. The pins and needles in my leg lessened and matured as I hobbled. The man chuckled at me and rode on, the bell sounding again as he left. I sat back down on the cold steps, my toes twitching with the sensation that was still faintly annoying me. I sat on the newspaper. It was just a fraction warmer.

The street began to take life, passers-by looked at me but marched on, their long dark clothes shielding them from the bitter wind. More bicycles bounced over the cobbled stone street, a shriek or a call from one boy to another. The mill was starting and the workers were making their dreary way.

A horse and cart thundered past at speed, the rider clipping the whip savagely to slow his horse. Lads on bicycles stumbled erratically and a few clattered to the street cobbles making the air blue.

When it was lighter a few of the windows had their curtains open. Quite a long way down the road I heard people's voices. They were saying goodbye and a woman was standing at a doorway waving as a man walked away. I remembered instantly my parents walking away. I had sat on the steps hours ago and waved at them as they left.

There was a noise, a loud noise. It came from behind me. The door was being opened. I froze, my mouth open with fear. I could hear the bolts being drawn back and a key turned in the lock. I contemplated running away but instead I stood up. I stepped back and watched as the door opened. It was really creaky and sounded like a scream as it was pushed back against the brick wall that had been my pillow.

'Oh, hello there,' a woman's voice said as the door swung open. Inside it was bright, much warmer, very light and big. I could hear children's voices. They were shouting at each other, happy playful yelps. 'Why don't you come in dear,' the woman said to me. I looked at her. She was about my mum's age, I thought, so she must have been ok. A long black skirt danced around her ankles and a tight blue blouse clung to her corseted, yet cuddly, torso. She had black shoes, which were about eye level to me as I'd stumbled down the steps into the street. She smiled at me and I fidgeted with my skirt. Suddenly I felt dirty and cold and still very tired. 'Come on dear, I'll get you some breakfast. You must be hungry.' I took a step towards her. 'This can be your home now. You'll like it, I promise. You'll make lots of new friends. Lots of children live here.'

I thought for a minute. I had no choice really and I was hungry and very cold. I remember charging in then, almost crashing into her and the door closed behind me.

As I sit here today I think back to the time when my parents abandoned me. It was only the beginning of a very long story. A story unfolded over time causing confusion, greed, unhappiness and money. It also bought some happiness, a little love and eventually some answers. The good points are always harder to find but they last a lot longer. I can barely remember their faces now, their features faded with each passing hour sat out there in the cold. After a week I could only just remember the outlines, the colour of their hair, the red coat my mother loved to wear and the back of the cart as the horses took them away, the echo of the hooves on the cobbled streets ringing out loudly. After a month I had forgotten that too and they remained in my memory very much as they do now, just there somehow but without faces.

It is January 1935 and a new year has begun. I shouldn't dwell on the past, especially my childhood but I find as the years drift by I think more and more about what might have been and less about what might still be to come. Everything seems so inevitable somehow.

Only last year the *Queen Mary* was launched. I desperately wanted to go on it. We could so easily afford it but Clarissa, my mother-in-law, claimed my animated talk of it was "wearing her to a shadow" so that was that. Perhaps one day I will get to go. Frederick said travel was unwise, especially at this time. I don't understand what he means but one never questions one's husband, not in public and certainly not in this house. He says the world has gone mad and we would be safer staying home. I am quite convinced you know that he wasn't so very weak when we met. In fact, his mother couldn't stand the sight of me; I'm sure, an orphan – for her son – never! And yet he told her plain as day he was going to marry me. Now he agrees with every word she blurts out. Clarissa never speaks, she commands, she tells, she orders, but she never asks.

There were riots in France last year, some nonsense about government corruption. "Most unsatisfactory", according to the oracle - Clarissa. Personally the news enthralled me, something with an edge, something rebellious... Why can't he see I'm dying of boredom here? I feel gloomy, neglected, unwanted. I feel sorry for myself. I am trapped you see. I am trapped in a situation that doesn't have an exit. I know; I've looked.

This won't do I tell myself. A telegram arrived yesterday announcing the arrival of Clarissa's sister for a fortnight; apparently she requires a change of air for her health. I have my suspicions she simply wishes to feed from someone else's income but perhaps it is best to be quiet on such matters. It is common knowledge that her husband has gambling debts.

The thought of two of them fills me with dread. I will have to find plenty of reasons to be absent for much of every day. I am sure that will not be satisfactory but I simply cannot tolerate Clarissa in double. Still, it could prove entertaining in a sadistic way; the two of them battling for command over the same teapot!

Again, this will not do I tell myself although I am reluctant to go downstairs. I have to get on with the day. Another day like the one just passed. Or maybe not... if I'm lucky something different might occur. I will pray for a miracle. One must never give up hope entirely.

Chapter Three

March 2009

'So, do you want me to start on the decorating or did you want some time?' Andy asked her. He sighed heavily, heaved another sack of peat into the back of his van and smiled at the memory of her face. The phone almost slipped from his grasp as he wrestled with the van door keys. The seven-thirty sunshine cloaked his driveway in a bright shine and Andy squinted from the glare.

'Are you alright?' Sophie sat on the stairs, the receiver cradled between her ear and shoulder, twiddling with the cord idly. Why hadn't she been able to get him off her mind? Whatever was wrong with her? It had been years since Joe and she hadn't suffered from any of these electric feelings since. Most inconvenient; considering she had hired the man.

'Oh yeah,' his breathing heavy. 'Just heaving some bags of peat around, sorry. There, that's that for now. So, what do you reckon?' he straightened up and moved away from the growing supplies stock.

'Um, I think we should get started. The police aren't interested in the house so I may as well get on with that whilst the garden is out of bounds. When are you free?' Sophie prayed for sooner rather than later. She missed him already, stupidly since she barely knew the man.

'How's tomorrow for you?' he asked, 'I could be with you early, that way we'd get through a lot in the day, good head start. Know what I mean?'

'Marvellous – shall we say eight a.m.? I have to work on Monday but I can help out during tomorrow and Sunday,' she purred huskily.

'Great, see you tomorrow Sophie, looking forward to it.'

'Me too,' she whispered. 'Now, I'd better go to work.' Today she really did have that Friday feeling.

Atwood Infants had taken Sophie on a year ago when she had finished university. It had been a good decision, the headmaster was a little old fashioned but he pretty much left them to it.

The school always reminded her of a rabbit warren, once you left the confines of the reception area from which the staff room, headmasters office, school reception office and toilets were, you entered the library and dining room with the kitchen. From that central point all classrooms lingered with their respective entrances and cloakrooms. There was nothing sweeter than the little named pegs and trays where the children kept their coats and outer shoes. The headmaster liked the children to leave their shoes with their coats and instructed all parents to provide plimsolls for inside the school. This, he claimed, kept things cleaner.

Each year group had its own entrance. The older the children were the messier their cloakrooms became! So too was that true of their behaviour. The great hall, that wasn't so very large once you returned as an adult, was also accessed from the central point of the dining room.

It was morning break time and as usual the headmaster wanted his ten-minute chat that always lasted at least fifteen. This meant they would have less than five minutes to actually sit back and relax before the second half of the morning commenced. The children were only young and some days it felt as if they had wind-up handles on their backs that were stuck on maximum velocity and top volume.

'If I could have a minute of your attention please,' the head master stood up, his full five feet and clung onto the lapels of his tweed jacket. He wore a forest green knitted tank top, and a checked shirt beneath his jacket that made him look like a cross between a country squire and an eccentric millionaire. Sophie exchanged a smile with Linda as they took their favourite seats.

'Here we go,' Linda mumbled, 'another speech of a lifetime, one day Michael Aspel will walk in.' Sophie giggled quietly and smoothed her skirt.

The room began to assemble into a chaotic order around them. The chairs were of slightly mismatched colour as if the supplier had run out of violet and thought no-one would notice if an odd number of them were actually lilac or pale grey. They were positioned in rows originally but inevitably ended up scattered into clusters of twos and threes; and were so worn out they could probably pass the history test better than the students. A hush befell the room as the headmaster rocked back and forth slowly on his heels.

'Ok, good morning,' he said, his voice far louder than you would expect for a man of his stature. 'I wanted to have a brief word with you all about the summer fete. As you know we always have a summer fete here at Atwood. I thought it would be nice to buck the trend,' he smirked and the teachers smiled in obedience at his pathetic attempt for a joke. 'Anyway,' he continued still rocking slightly, 'this year the local theatre have offered us their mobile stage and I thought it would be rather nice to put on a little play for the parents.' A smattering of expression floated around the room like a mist. The head master surveyed the faces happily, his fingers tapping on his rotund stomach as he swayed. 'Sophie,' he said suddenly.

Sophie looked up sharply. It wasn't his custom to single people out and it unnerved them whenever he did.

'Yes?'

'As our resident and most qualified English teacher I thought you'd like to direct our little production. You can choose a play; any play will do but try to find one with an Easter theme. Can you do that?'

'Yes I should think,' Sophie said, nodding her head. 'Why Easter?'

'Like I said, I'd like to buck the trend. After all, we've just concluded the term leading to Easter and I thought the children created some quite exceptional artwork when they came back after the break.'

'Yes of course, ok,' Sophie agreed. 'What about the students, will they audition or shall we pick a class to take the parts?'

'Are they old enough to audition?' he asked, gazing around the room to indicate it was an open forum now. He lifted his chin offering the teachers an unwanted view of his nostrils. 'Any thoughts?' he pressed.

'Nah, they're too young,' chipped in Glenis, the plumpest PE teacher Sophie had ever seen in her life. 'Give them each a little part and maybe a song or two so they can all have a go at the end.' Glenis's red cheeks glowed like a fire. Sophie wondered if she would blow up as she watched Glenis collect another two chocolate chip cookies from the central coffee table and stuff them into her ample mouth at once. It was a gift, really it was, an art form in its own right.

'All in favour?' the headmaster raised his right hand. How democratic, thought Sophie. A chorus of non-committal yes's went around the room. 'Right then, Sophie my dear, pick the class with the most active children in it and we'll have a few from there for the lead parts. The entire lower form can join in the sing song at the end. Pat, can you handle the choir please?'

'Yes sir,' Pat, an elderly music teacher on the verge of retirement, nick-named by some of the older children as Postman, although thankfully he seemed oblivious to the fact.

'Great, let's get started then. Sophie, Pat, give me an update will you, this time next week say?'

'Of course head master,' boomed Pat. Sophie nodded at him quietly.

'Ok, that's all for now. Thank you folks, have a good day.' The headmaster sauntered off towards the coffee percolator and poked around with the mugs. Despite being one of the longest serving at the school he still managed to get lost when it came to locating the sugar and milk.

'Right, you, spill!' Linda's clasped her hands around Sophie's the second the headmaster took a step from his post.

'Well hello to you too, how are you Sophie, I'm fine thanks' Sophie mocked, giggling. Linda gave her an arched eyebrow and a stern wagging finger. 'What?'

'Spill, something's eating you, now what is it?'

'It's nothing, really,' she insisted, knowing full well that Linda would not cave. The room was noisy, the other teachers gossiping about the headmaster's latest trial hairpiece and the alleged affair between the absent geography teacher and the caretaker.

'Nothing eh. You're glowing girl, now are you going to tell me or am I going to have to drag it out of ya?' Linda took a large sip of her morning black coffee. 'Oh lovely, they ration this you know. How am I supposed to get through all these ridiculous emotional hurdles without my coffee? I ask you!' Linda rested her hands on her bump affectionately. 'Can't wait, honestly. Enough about me, spill!'

Sophie smiled at her, took another sip of her tea and fiddled with her notes for her next lesson. English, the year three students, aged seven at most and more highly strung than the circus. They would probably be best for the play she thought. It could be very hard going at times but she wouldn't swap her job for anything. Some of the younger ones were adorable.

'I'm waiting!' Linda said, 'come on, we've got like five minutes before that damned bell goes. Sophie sighed and smiled at Linda. She was her best friend and Sophie couldn't have gotten through the Joe nightmare without her. Frustratingly she saw straight through her every time and sometimes it was just nice to keep a secret.

'Ok but it wasn't that good. We found skeletons in my new garden and the police say there are two of them.' Sophie watched Linda's face carve into the O shape of surprise. 'See I told you it wasn't that good,' she smiled and flipped her papers back into the blue folder.

'Who's we?' Linda perked up immediately, her long auburn hair swaying excitedly. Sophie giggled at her.

'Has anyone ever told you you're impossible?' rising to exit the staff room in preparation for the challenge that was class 3C.

'Oh yeah, tons of times,' Linda swished her hand at Sophie. 'So?'

'I hired a gardener and decorator, same guy, he does everything,' she felt the blush glowing already. What was that?

'Oh yeah, I bet he does by the way you look. Have you?'

'What? Are you mad, I just met him yesterday,' she said indignantly, giving Linda her hand and yanking her up from the low seat.

The bell tolled loudly and Sophie cringed at the sound. You would think after a whole year of listening to it at least six times a day she would have got used to it by now.

'So, true love,' Linda breathed heavily on the ascent, 'never did run smooth apparently,' she gasped. 'Thanks. And anyway, if it's meant to be why wait!'

'You can talk,' Sophie giggled, 'Mrs I'm-never-going-to-marry-him!'

'Well that's different,' Linda, towering a few feet above Sophie, wagged her finger again. 'Just as well I did marry the bugger isn't it!' she tapped her unborn baby tenderly. 'A girl can change her mind you know, woman's provocative, don't forget.' Sophie smiled at her as they headed for the door amidst the throng of the other teachers. Sophie glanced at the white board that displayed this week's timetable as she passed. The year six's were out the next afternoon at District Sports. That meant a quiet afternoon – good news for all concerned.

'Keep me posted,' Linda said, 'don't be shy, could be just what you need,' she smiled, 'seriously, just think about it.'

'I can't help but think about him,' Sophie said in a hushed voice. 'Catch ya later,' she winked and Linda laughed.

Sophie was looking forward to going home, having collected various paint charts from Focus in her lunch break she was planning to pour over them and choose colours ready to go shopping with Andy in the morning.

The next morning Sophie rose at 6 a.m. wide awake. She showered for what felt like ages, scrubbed her entire body until it glistened pink, washed and rinsed her hair twice, and lavished coconut body-milk on in spades. As she lay naked on the freshly crisp bed sheets, the cream sinking into her skin, she thought about his imminent arrival. It was ridiculous but she felt instantly ready for him the moment she thought about him, her body wanted him, the desire melted from her abundantly. She had to do something about it, stop thinking about him, buy herself a new dress, or something. Anything would do, but definitely something.

It was almost time for him to arrive. She got dressed, thinking about what she wore for the first time in the past three years.

The doorbell rang as she dabbed musk perfume behind her ears. The scarlet shade she was beginning to learn to live with returned to her face as she floated happily down the stairs to open the front door.

'Good morning,' she smiled, widening the door to allow him to enter. 'Do you want a cup of tea or shall we head straight out to the shops?'

'I'm ok if you are,' he grinned at her. 'Whenever you're ready we'll set off.' She smiled coyly at him and gestured towards the lounge. Andy took the hint and settled onto the sofa. He looked so nice in her living room she thought lazily leaning at the door frame.

'I see you've arranged the furniture,' he said, 'last time I was here it was sort of jumbled up in the middle like,' he flashed her another winning smile.

'Yeah, I thought I should. Shouldn't have bothered I guess since we'll have to move it now,' she laughed. 'Let me get my shoes, I'll just be a minute…'

'No rush,' he said. Within minutes Sophie was climbing into Andy's van. It wasn't elegant but thankfully she'd thought to wear jeans for the occasion.

'Have you picked out colours then?' he asked as he drove them to the shop. The van was littered with papers, colour charts, flipcharts with client records, supply orders and despatch notices. 'Sorry about the mess, the van is sort of like my office too since my spare room is for my daughter,' he said.

Sophie sprung a glance at him. Daughter...now that she hadn't seen coming.

'There are some colour charts down there,' he indicated the glove compartment, 'if you want to check.' Sophie was still watching him, the scarlet shade paling. 'Sophie, did you hear? The colours...'

'Oh yes,' she shook herself to life. 'I picked already,' she said, fiddling anxiously through her large handbag for the charts that she'd crammed into the little available space earlier that morning. Daughter... was he married after all?

'Good, what'd you go for?' he risked a casual smile at her and turned back to the road. Sophie was still fiddling through her bag, staring into it desperately seeking an answer, either that or for it to open up and swallow her whole.

'I know it's in here somewhere,' she whispered. 'Just give me a minute...'

Andy drove on in silence. The sun was beginning to rise and he flipped the shade down above his eyes. The traffic was quiet this early in the day. Happily he began to hum, which irritated Sophie unreasonably. How could he be happy with someone else and leave her feeling like this?

'Don't worry Sophie,' he said as she fumbled anxiously into the depths of her bag. He watched her sigh heavily and twiddle her thumbs. 'We'll sort it when we get there.' She smiled quickly to show willing and gazed out the window. Maybe she had jumped to conclusions. *Pull yourself together* she mentally chastised.

'So, you have a daughter,' she said matter-of-factly. 'You never said,' she accused. The confusion spread over Andy's face visibly.

'Um yeah, sorry, look it won't get in the way of the job,' he glared at her sceptically. 'She doesn't live with me all the time.'

'Oh I know, I mean of course, I'm just surprised,' she said, recovering, 'that's all. How old is she?' she asked in a voice that she hoped masked the instant prickly edge caused by the news. Why was it important anyway, she took a deep breath and counted to ten. *Get a grip.*

'She's only six,' he smiled, 'nearly seven. Annabel, she's sweet, I think you'd like her a lot,' he gushed. 'She's beautiful, clearly doesn't get that from me,' he laughed.

An extraordinary concoction of admiration and fear engulfed her in a moment. Andy was gorgeous so if the little girl had inherited her looks from her mother that would make her mother a super-model type. If that was Andy's type it gave her absolutely no chance whatsoever. On the other hand, it was sweet of him to be modest about himself and wonderful to see how much he clearly adored his daughter.

'Six you say, I may know her,' Sophie realised as soon the words tumbled out her mouth. 'Where does she go to school?'

'Atwood Infants,' he said shortly. 'You don't have kids do you?' his eyebrows raised quizzically as he turned quickly from the road to look at her. They were slowing for a traffic light.

'No, no, but I'm a teacher,' she said, 'at Atwood.' She felt better that they were on safe territory again. Andy's face lit up.

'You're kidding! I had you down as an office worker, not sure why. You just seem so organised, except the bag incident of course,' he laughed. She managed a small laugh in response. Her insides felt like jelly and her heart felt as if it had relocated to her mouth. All she wanted to do was scream at him; are you married? Are you taken? It was driving her insane. *Get a grip, get a grip, get a grip...*

'She does go there; you probably do know her then. What a small world,' he marvelled as he drove them into the car park of the DIY store and yanked up the handbrake. It creaked like a torque wrench and she leapt slightly. It had been ages since she had been this jumpy.

The car park was crammed with white vans, some decorated on the sidewalls and others plain. A couple of pick-up trucks and a few builders' flatbed trucks were parked haphazardly by the main doors.

'Tradesman's hour,' Andy explained at her lost gaze. 'Shall we?' he smiled at her and was around by her door before she had even gathered up her littered handbag, helped her down carefully and looked into her eyes. For a moment they stood suspended between the seat and the door. Sophie's heart melted back into place. If only he were available.

'Let's go shopping,' she whispered. Andy still had hold of her hand as he closed the van door and led her towards the shop. It felt nice, she thought, his fingers entwined in hers.

'I think we'll need a trolley,' he said, reluctantly letting her hand trail away. 'We'll need quite a lot of paint. Have you got your colour list?' Sophie nodded at him in silence and headed on into the shop.

It was a big shop, a warehouse really but with shelves. Sophie trailed after him, guided by his experience. My God, she thought, I'd need a map to find my way around here by myself.

'I'm going for lilac in the bedroom,' she told him, 'a pale blue in the other rooms upstairs, and either milk chocolate or cream in the lounge. I don't think we need worry about the kitchen and bathroom since my Grandmother only had them decorated with the new fitments last year.'

'Good plan,' he said, 'we'll be able to get a better deal by doubling up the colours upstairs,' he pushed the trolley towards the paint tins. 'This way,' he inclined his head. She followed him dreamily. *New plan, she thought, forget the potential problems and focus on the here and now. You'll probably never see him again after this anyway so just enjoy his company whilst it lasts.*

'So how long have you been a teacher?' he asked, lifting down two tins and holding them before her. She pointed to the one in his left hand and watched him load two of the larger size into the trolley with a thud.

'I started at Atwood a year ago now,' she said, 'I was at university up until then. It's quite a long course,' she said, 'but worth it in the end.'

'How long?'

'Well there are two options really but I did the four-year,' she explained, a brief smile playing at her lips.

'Do you have to teach everything or just the one topic?'

'At infants you have to teach everything but I focused on English, language and literature. I mainly teach English and a little drama. When you get your job you find that the other teachers have preferences too so you can just teach your favourite topics for about two thirds of the time. Of course there's a lot of learning to read and write with the younger children.' Andy nodded in agreement and spun the trolley around skilfully, narrowly avoiding the other tradesman in the aisle.

'Yeah, my Annabel is a good reader; probably thanks to you I expect,' he smiled as he manoeuvred the trolley around a corner.

'Don't we need brushes and rollers?' she queried, as they appeared to be leaving the paint tins behind.

'Nah, I've got loads of them in the van. Which blue do you prefer?' he held up two, 'remember they'll dry darker.'

'The sky one I think,' she decided, 'no, the cornflower.' Andy juggled the tins a little and laughed. 'Or there's that one over there,' he nosed towards the shelf.

'No, the sky one,' she nodded, her hair bouncing in agreement. Andy watched her eyes sparkling and plonked two further tins into the trolley.

'What about the landing, hallway and stairs?'

'I'll go with cream,' she told him. 'Boring I know but it'll be fresh.'

'Good choice, we'll get extra just in case it needs another coat.' The trolley was looking decidedly heavy. 'I think we're done here,' he said. 'I'll just get an extra dust sheet or two and we'll make a start.'

The van rattled along the road comfortably and Sophie was beginning to feel more relaxed, she could either forget about the potential disaster looming over her; the fact that she had fallen in love with an unobtainable man, or she could quiz him during the weekend to ascertain the truth. The problem with her quizzing skills was that she always ended up looking downright nosy, which had the opposite effect to the one she desired, and made people clam up.

'I think you owe me a life story,' he suddenly announced, laughing at her puzzlement. 'I distracted you the other day with my life story and now it's your turn, as we drive home, well your home obviously.' They were heading through the town centre and the traffic was waking up to the weekend. People had surfaced since their outbound journey.

'Oh really?' Sophie chuckled, 'I see, don't mince your words will you,' she mocked. 'It's not that interesting I'm afraid. I may bore you to tears.'

'I'll risk it,' he quipped. 'Fire away!'

Sophie felt the scarlet blush on the ascent again and quickly looked out the passenger window to deflect his noticing it. The sun caught her eye so she had to look back at him, wiped a tear from the direct sunlight away.

'Ok well here goes. I grew up in Keyes,' she said, 'my mum and dad still live there. They didn't have me until they were in their forties and I was, well, unplanned.' Andy laughed lightly, a grin growing on his handsome face. 'School was in Atwood so they had to drive me to and fro every day but they never seemed to mind. I stayed on at school for the sixth form, took my A-levels and went to university in Cambridge.'

'Cambridge? Wow, you must be really smart,'

'Why?'

'I read somewhere that you had to be real clever to get into Oxford or Cambridge,' he laughed.

'Really? I don't think so, no more than anywhere else,' she protested.

'When did you leave?' he asked, his smile tantalising her.

'I qualified year before last and started at Atwood Infants in the September. I did buy a little house in Keyes until grandmother left me this one but I sold it last month. Sweet little place, sad to move out really, but here is much closer to the school and I know she would have wanted me to live here.'

The same red traffic light that halted them earlier now lit up brightly as Andy slowed the van behind a string of multicoloured cars. The sun's beam was gathering strength as it rose and promised to be a pleasant day.

'Your grandmother didn't leave the house to your parents then, that's unusual,' he commented with a friendly smile.

'No, she told dad apparently, before she died, that she wanted me to have it. They already have their own place naturally. I never knew anything about it until after the funeral.' Sophie's mind clouded over with memories from the funeral, her face stained in grief momentarily and she hid a sly tear. Andy watched her quietly and indicated left into her road.

'Is university as wild as they say?' he wondered, changing tack. 'Sometimes I wish I had gone but I don't really think it would have suited me.'

'It's wild if you want it to be I suppose,' she contemplated, 'like most things in life you make it yours. I had some fun, had a pretty awful experience too, but overall it was the right thing to do. I never wanted to go further away. Cambridge was far enough. At least I could make it home easily for weekends and holidays.'

'So you lived in?' Andy rolled the van forwards as the amber lit up.

'Only during the week; the commute would have made it impossible.'

'What was so awful?' he asked, 'the exams?'

'No, the exams are hard yes, but if you've studied hard enough then it's ok. It was er, something else,' she wondered whether it was worthwhile telling him about Joe. She may never see him again and some things were best left unsaid. It had irked her that every time she told the story she came across as a bitter resentful cow. Flattering it wasn't, and whether she saw him again or not, she definitely didn't want him left with that impression of her.

'Sorry, you don't have to say,' he said quietly. 'Didn't mean to pry.' He pulled the van up in her driveway. 'We're here anyway,' he smiled, 'lets unload the paint.'

They painted for hours, chatting as they worked happily. It was time for a cup of tea. As she descended the stairs a hand-delivered envelope fell onto the mat. The envelope was typed neatly stating her name but no address beneath it. How strange. She dashed to the living room window but no-one was in sight. How very odd she thought, taking it into the kitchen and flicking the kettle switch on.

Her heart skipped a beat as she slid open the white envelope and unfolded the crisp white sheet of A4. Cut-out newspaper letters were messily pasted across the page.

I KNOW WHO YOU ARE. I'M WATCHING YOU. DON'T UPSET ME OR I MIGHT GET ANGRY AND YOU DON'T WANT ME TO DO THAT. OBEY ME. REMEMBER, DON'T UPSET ME. I HATE GETTING ANGRY.

Her shaky fingers released the sheet. It dropped like a lead balloon onto the table top, the heavy glue on the page making it fall like a hailstone. The sweat on her palms and her forehead sprang from her insides like the liquid from a shaken fizzy drinks can. Her eyes darted from the kitchen window to the front door. Who was watching her?

The hand that delivered it had slipped back into the unknown without detection.

'You have to go to the police with this,' Andy insisted, taking the envelope and letter from her and tossing them onto the bottom stair in disgust.

'Yes, I know,' she sighed. 'I will.'

'Promise?'

'Yes, I promise.' Sophie attempted a smile and sank into his offered embrace. There were times when living alone had its disadvantages.

Chapter Four

We had an argument yesterday, Frederick and I. He said he didn't want any children. I am devastated and have been crying all day, hiding my tears from him as best as I can. I feel sure that before we married he said he was keen on the idea. The same old subject yet again. I always lose. He is a stout man and I am much afraid of pushing my argument too far…I wouldn't stand a chance. Sometimes I think I am being ridiculous but when he raises his voice his face flushes a shade of red I can't say I've ever witnessed anywhere else, and his knuckles go white with the force of his fingers sinking into his palms with rage. It is when we reach this point that I retreat. One day I may attack but so far I've lacked courage at the sight of him. When he tosses dinner plates at the wall and I watch the discarded meal sliding down the paintwork I know poor Betsy will have to clean it up; trouble is there is nobody to clean me up if I were launched at the ever-suffering paintwork. I don't imagine even our never-complaining Betsy would go that far for her meagre salary.

The whole thing has made me think about the children's home again. Perhaps this diary is a bad idea but the doctor said it would be good for me to release my emotions. Better than pills he said, so I carry on. Clarissa says my doctor is one of those modern "progressive" doctors and won't hear a word against her own tyrannical doctor who in my opinion shouldn't be practising medicine on stuffed toys, let alone human beings.

Today Clarissa has gone out to coffee with a friend of hers who lives two streets away. They sit at the Lyons tea shop and lick iced buns, sip at expensive china cups of tea and discuss the waste of the youth today – namely me and whoever else they can think to disgrace publicly without threat of objection from the passers-by. It is acceptable to publicly dress-down one's daughter-in-law when she has come from unknown parentage. In fact, it is expected. Clarissa undertakes her duties as a lady with the utmost vigour. I can imagine them if I try.

"Why Clarissa my dear, how awful it must be for you to live under the same roof with one such as Elise. I mean, her dress, her simple lack of prosperity!"

"Yes indeed, you know she wears soft collars!"

"No! Shameful! Oh dear..." Then "kindly do not interrupt me my girl," to the waitress, "do be quiet whilst I'm talking to you, child."

Her sister's stay was a complete nightmare. I swear I all but went mad with the strain of the pair of them. It was so bad that I begged Katie to visit; our neighbour. She is the most wonderful woman, such a lovely person to live next door to. Her nephew was staying with her, such a treat, a lovely lad in his early twenties. Regrettably, upon introduction, his cheery greeting of "whatho all" was reprimanded by Clarissa with "kindly do not address me using such foul language boy". Overcome with complete embarrassment I suggested a walk in the pleasant sunshine, knowing full well that Clarissa and her clone would decline.

Katie – bless her – and her nephew were kind enough to pay little attention to my mother-in-law's rudeness but I must say, I shall never attempt society in her midst again.

Frederick has gone, as usual, to his club – Coates - for lunch and will remain there until he has had sufficient intoxication. It is a gentleman's club and naturally I have never set foot inside the door though I am led to believe that they frequently practice cricket and golf with the use of the bread rolls acting as balls. Apparently one's badminton skills are vastly improved by attempting to shoot the netted bobbin into the upturned ceiling lights. I imagine a sea of tweed-jacketed gentleman adopting the most appalling behaviour and casually stepping out into the street as if they had just vacated church itself.

He will return home for dinner whereupon the whole terrible argument may easily resume if I am not highly cautious. Betsy is very good about the whole dinner down the wall scenario. I often attempt to clean it up for her but she will have none of it.

"No mom, what if madam should see you cleaning it up?" and quite right she is too. My mother-in-law would utter something like "I am most seriously displeased with you Elise, you should be well aware that a man has every right to throw his own meal at his own wall without contradiction from his wife, your actions here go against your husband's will. Why, I am not surprised, a girl of your connections – whatsoever they may be!"

In the summer of 1900 I was five. I was living at the children's home where my parents had left me the previous year. Apparently they had been tracing my parents but no-one had come back to claim me so I guessed they hadn't been found.

I remember the room. It was big, the ceiling a lifetime high and the walls a pale creamy colour. The window went from the ceiling almost to the floor. The house must have been very old. It was always bright, airy and sometimes a little chilly. The curtains were almost always drawn back and the light spread across the floor like a fan, its colours spanning out on the balding carpet like a dance hall glitter ball.

I was playing with a doll. She was not really my doll but I liked to think she was. She had long blonde hair and wore a long pink ball gown. She was always going to a party, looking nice, always going somewhere exciting. I liked this notion. I always played the same game. I called her Cindy and she slept beside me at night. Mrs Betty never minded. She said it was nice to cuddle things at night. Mrs Betty was very nice. She was always there when I needed something. There were other ladies but I liked Mrs Betty best. She reminded me of my mum in almost every way.

'Hey, I want Cindy, it's my turn.' Rosie tried to take Cindy away from me. Her little fingers were stuck around Cindy's legs with a vice-like grip. Rosie was about my age. I remember screaming quite violently in protest.

'No, no, no,' I screamed. 'No, no.' I began to cry I think. My sobs were instant and full bodied. I didn't want to let Cindy go but Rosie was strong and quite insistent. I cried again, louder that time.

Rosie was wearing a smock style dress, forest green with button detail to the v-neckline. She had dark hair and olive skin. To me she was exotic but on this particular day she was plain mean. I didn't allow her to take Cindy from me. I continued to yelp until Mrs Betty approached us.

'Hey, what's going on here then?' Mrs Betty approached us quickly, her strong quick strides brought her to us in mere seconds. I remember her round legs coming closer and closer to me like stumps on a cricket pitch. Her shoes sounded heavy as they thumped on the floor, the vibrations rang through my ears. By this time I was on the floor and Rosie and I were fighting over Cindy.

'Rosie! Leave that doll alone. Can't you see that Elise is playing with that? Here,' she dragged Rosie to her feet with one swift movement and I clutched Cindy to my chest protectively. 'Come with me.' Mrs Betty and Rosie left. Rosie wined as she was marched away. I hugged Cindy tightly. I had won, but only for the moment. Rosie would be back. She always came back. Furtively I glanced around at the other children but they all quickly resumed their own playful activities. There was no further threat to Cindy so convinced, I continued my imaginary party, Cindy had a ball to go to, looking stunning like Cinderella. I was too young to realise the implications of my games of course.

At night I slept fitfully, occasionally waking, my nightdress soaked with tears. Mrs Betty kept muttering about getting Sigmund Freud's new book; *The Interpretation of Dreams*. She muttered about nightmares and magical cures. 'It's revolutionary,' she maintained as I sobbed into a hanky and eventually fell asleep in her arms.

Although the children's home was not *my home* it become as such and even though I was a child at the time I remember watching Mrs Betty and the other carers and thinking how kindly they looked upon us children. It must have been a very rewarding occupation, to care for a child, an innocent young child. What a pleasure to help a child grow into a well-behaved, kind and helpful person, to be there, at their side during each stage of their upbringing.

I'm sorry dear diary but I really do wish Frederick would consent to us having a family of our own. I can think of no other greater joy I can bring to life. A child would give us, or at least me, such meaning, such happiness… perhaps one day it will happen regardless, although I am not delighted at the prospect of entertaining Frederick in my bed of a night. The outcome would be worth any torment from him in that respect. He seems to have no desires of that nature these days and although I mourn the loss of my dream of motherhood, I am thankful all the same.

Chapter Five

March 2009

Sophie picked up the phone on the third ring, happily tucked it beneath her ear and splashed a splodge of lilac paint onto the bedroom wall. Paul Weller sang out of the radio to them as they worked in compatible silence, covering the bedroom walls in record time.

'Hellooo,' she sang, large brush strokes of lilac blossoming out like wild lavender.

'Miss Harris?'

'Yes,'

'Its Suffolk Constabulary,' a low voice announced. Sophie stopped painting and rested the brush on the edge of the tin. Andy glanced over at her casually.

'Yes,' she said

'It's about the skeletons. We're having a little trouble identifying them. Is there any way you can provide us with a list of the previous house-owners? You should find the information on the house deeds,' the constable informed her. Sophie watched Andy who was still painting, wondered how she could delay his departure.

'Miss Harris?'

'Oh yes, sorry. Yes of course, I'll draw up a list and drop it into the station next week,' she promised.

'Oh that would be great. Thank you Miss Harris. We would normally do it, but we're so understaffed at the moment...'

'I understand, is there anything else?'

'No, that's all, except you may like to know we've dated the year of death to early or mid thirties.'

'Oh really? How can you tell?'

'Simple really,' the constable went on, 'the shoes in particular were made by a firm that went out of business in 1941. The batch numbers on the soles were still clearly legible believe it or not. Good shoes those, not cheap. Still new at the time of burial we think. We managed to trace the batch the shoes came from, since they were part of a line that ceased manufacturer in 1936. They had to have been purchased before that. Quite a popular style back in the day,' the constable beamed, his grin bearing down the line like an impression. 'Seems to be making a come back, the t-bar type, my Mrs got some only the other day,' he waffled on.

'Wow,' Sophie said. 'That's amazing.'

'Yes Miss, red she bought, just like these ones. Anyway that's it for now. See you next week then Miss Harris, with the house owners, goodbye.' The constable replaced the phone and the line clicked off. Slowly she sank down to the floor against the last unpainted wall.

'Taking a break?' Andy cast her a smile and continued with his vast professional strokes. She nodded silently and fiddled with a stray strand of hair. 'What's up?'

'The police want a list of the ex-owners of this place,' she sighed.

'So, you have that don't you?' he asked, his eyes still fixated on the smooth finish of the painting.

'Yeah,' she sighed again. 'It's just that if it really is tied up with a previous owner then it's definitely connected to my family.'

'Ah, I see,' Andy nodded in understanding. 'Tainted Love' drifted from the radio speaker now as Andy released his brush and came to sit beside her. 'Can I help?' he patted her knee and clasped it with his fingers. She smiled at him.

'Thanks but I reckon I need to do this bit alone.' Andy nodded in response and pulled her to her feet.

'I'll carry on here,' he said, 'call me if you need any help.'

'Thank you,' she said, 'you should be careful, you're becoming indispensable!' Sophie cradled his fingers inside hers and squeezed his hand. 'I'd better get the deeds out,' she said, 'I'll be downstairs.'

Sophie shivered again; it was horrible to think that a dead body had been planted inches beneath the lawn, even if it was a long time ago. A good sixty to seventy years ago, the police had assured her. If they were right the house was definitely in her family at the time. She wondered if her grandmother knew about the body in the garden...wouldn't that be something you would normally mention? Maybe she had known that Sophie would live in it and do something with the garden...one day a hole would be dug and the bones would be found...one day it would all be discovered. And today was that day, she thought gloomily.

'What are you thinking?' Andy cut into her thoughts, appearing in the kitchen doorway like a dream.

'Why didn't anybody mention it,' she asked as if Andy should have known. 'I mean you don't normally leave people houses complete with dead owners do you?'

'So you think that it's an ex-owner of this place?'

'Well yes, don't you?'

'I'm not so sure,' Andy admitted. 'I think you should leave it to the police, you'll only worry yourself silly otherwise.' She nodded silently in agreement. A few moments of silence prevailed. However did he know her so well after such a short acquaintance?

Sophie unleashed the rolled-up sleeves of her cashmere sweater and they slid down her arms covering the goose pimples from the cool air. Her long eyelashes fluttered over her hazel eyes, the worry beginning to sparkle in them like fireworks.

'Just getting some more water,' he said lifting the bucket to the kitchen sink. 'Got to sugar soap the last wall,' he explained and turned the taps on full. Sophie sat at the kitchen table for a moment then slid into the lounge and pulled out the house deeds from the box in the far corner. She had to face the music.

Neatly Sophie began to compile a list:

Previous owners of 26 Convent Avenue, Atwood

Current owner: I, Sophie Harris, inherited the house this year – 2009 – from my grandmother upon her death on 17th January 2009.

Previous owner: Katherine Harris – my grandmother – inherited the house from her parents, Rodney and Katherine Harris on their death. Rodney Harris died in 1978, his wife Katherine nee Christie died in 1976. Katherine Harris occupied the house from 1978 until her death in January 2009.

One from last owner: Rodney Harris inherited the house in 1964 from his elder brother, Frederick Harris, upon his death.

Two from last owner: Frederick, as the elder son, had been left the house by their parents, upon their early death in 1909.

This is where the records cease.

So, one of the list entries could be a murderer. To make matters worse someone out there knew about it – the poison pen – they must know. Otherwise, why write to her at all? A violent shiver swept through her again, making her blood run cold. It was simply horrible. She folded the paper and slid it into a cream envelope, wrote *police* on the front and ran up the stairs in search of distraction that came in the form of decorating and the dreamy presence of Andy himself.

The coffee shop was crowded and noisy. From the till Sophie spied Linda crushing her way amongst the shoppers, in a race for the last tiny free table as the current occupants were gathering their plastic carriers with difficulty.

'Excuse me,' she called in desperate fear that another couple were bustling towards it faster than her seven-month pregnant form could carry her. 'Excuse me, but I really need that table, I've simply got to sit down, I'm sorry.'

'Oh, no, that's fine, please,' the man drew back the chair for her.

'Thank you so much, thank you,' Linda was at the point of the fifth thank you by the time Sophie reached her with the tray. The couple had gone into the jungle of chairs to find another table.

A sharp blast of air release spat from the coffee percolator loudly. The waitress clattered by with a loaded tray of stacked coffee mugs. The aroma filled the air, infused with the sugar icing from the cakes, and wafted sweetly amongst the murmur of chatter that lingered above the tables like a cloud.

'You can't keep pulling that one you know,' she laughed. 'That's like the third time today!'

'Hey, I'm genuine,' she protested comically and rested her hands on her growing baby. 'Besides, my back is killing me. I swear, this baby will be the death of me.'

'Don't be so dramatic,' Sophie giggled, pouring out the tea from the leaking teapot. 'Anyway, you shouldn't say such things.' She sank her teeth into the coffee cake. Linda watched her enviously.

'You may as well, you'll be dieting anyway in a couple of months.'

'Yeah well, I'll be dieting twice as long if I don't watch it now won't I. Anyway, what's up with you? There's a look about you today, you know you can't hide from me. Spill!' Linda commanded, sipping her coffee.

'It's nothing really, I promise.' Sophie rested her giant cup down on the saucer that was larger than her side plates at home, and looked at Linda who eyed her cautiously. 'Ok, ok, I was just thinking about Joe.'

Linda nearly spat her coffee out. An elderly man at the next table looked at them suspiciously but Linda clearly didn't care.

'Why?' She put her cup down on the table with a clatter. 'Whatcha want think about that prize prat for?' she demanded, her voice rising. Sophie hushed her and the elderly man stared at them in disdain. Half laughing she took another sip of coffee.

'I meant whether or not I should mention it to Andy, you know, if things were...' her voice trailed into the distance along with her thoughts. Linda snapped her fingers and flashed Sophie a smile.

'Oh yeah, what's happened?' She leant forward eagerly on the table, 'did you kiss him yet?' she whispered. 'I bet you kissed him, you've gone all coy on me.'

'No, no, nothing like that, but, well you know,' she flushed pink. 'Should I mention Joe or not?'

'Only if the conversation crops up, otherwise not a word! The idiot's got nothing on you anymore kid so forget him. If you end up dating this Andy then the topic of the past will come up naturally and you can handle it then. For God's sake don't say anything now. It'll just look, well, rehearsed if you know what I mean.'

'Yes I suppose you're right,' she agreed with a sigh.

'I'm always right,' Linda said sternly and giggled. 'So, do I know him?'

'Actually you may do, he has a daughter at the school. Annabel, I think she's in one of your classes.' Sophie watched Linda's mind whirl into action.

'Oh yes!' Linda said, 'I know her, sweet little thing...ah, are you sure about the name?'

'Yes, why?'

'Oh honey,' Linda sighed. 'Did he tell you he was married?' Linda watched the colour fade from Sophie's face. 'I'm sorry honey, I'm really sorry. I could be wrong, but Annabel's parents are definitely still together. I thought they were happy, I guess you don't know what's behind closed doors though.' Linda babbled as Sophie took a gulp of her steaming coffee and gasped as the burn in her throat travelled south. 'I'm sorry,' Linda whispered finally.

'I should have known,' Sophie said. 'I really should have known.' She tossed her unfinished coffee cake on the tray; her appetite vanished.

'Are you going to eat that?' Linda asked. 'Sorry.' Sophie half smiled at her.

'Go ahead, I've had enough,' she said and watched Linda dig into the remainder of cake with obvious delight. 'So, how are you doing? How'd you get on at the clinic last week?'

64

'Good,' she mumbled, swallowing the cake almost whole. 'This really is good cake. You're right, to hell with the diet. I'm already fat anyway!' she giggled.

'The clinic?'

'Yeah, sorry, it was all right. They said my blood pressure is up a bit.'

'But you didn't have high blood pressure before...'

'Yeah, I did, it's just gone up a fraction more but it's ok, really, I've got to have scans every four weeks, that's all it means. They called me "high risk"' she mimicked her fingers into speech marks with a chuckle. 'Really honey, don't worry about me, apparently loads of pregnant woman have high blood pressure.'

Sophie nodded at her and drained the last of her coffee.

'I suppose you get more scan pictures,' she tried to be upbeat but the news of Andy's marriage was stuck in her mind like a stain.

The house was the same as always. Sophie took a seat on the floral settee and smiled at her mother as she accepted the cup of tea. It had been too long since she had come home to visit. She always left it too long and her mother always made tea. Even now, she thought, she really wanted something else other than to simply see how her parents were. Did that make her ungrateful? She didn't think so but then she wouldn't.

When she thought back to the winter evenings her parents drove her back and forth to her friends' houses in Atwood streaks of guilt ripped through her. She should really try harder, after everything they had done for her. Further guilt tormented her when she remembered that they had nothing from her grandmother's death and she had everything. Difficult as it may be. She had still been the chosen one. Was there any logic to any of it she wondered?

Now, settled in their retirement and living amongst other retired couples Keyes was perfect for her parents, but then it always had been. As a child, especially one of few children, Keyes had never felt exactly exciting for Sophie. The peace and quiet was something she had grown into, rather than appreciated whilst she had it.

It was Sunday and that meant her parents had just returned home from the regular church ceremony, pausing for a roast dinner at the local pub on route.

'The walk does us both a power of good,' her mother enthused, tea in hand. 'Food is always good there too; you should come over one day. It'll be fun,' her mother continued, 'don't worry, you can skip the church part if you like,' she smiled. 'So, how are you settling in?'

She noticed her father's watchful gaze. He had always been a steady person her father, always on the lookout and always in the background just waiting to leap into action. These days he hardly looked ready to leap anywhere with his woollen patterned knitwear and brown corduroy trousers, but then he was retired. Her mother was no better in badly designed dresses that did nothing to flatter her. At what point did people lose the sense to coordinate clothing she wondered. Retirement seemed to catch everyone the same way. It turned people into clones of the generation before them.

'It's been somewhat difficult with the police tearing up the garden but I'm coping now.'

'What police?' Her father's voice was stern and stronger than she had heard it in months. He stood by the fireplace, his stance lacking the strength he once had but remaining the picture of control. Sophie scanned his features, now a little wrinkled by his eyes but they still held a power. She watched the colour drain from her father's face like the sun from a dusk sky. He knew. He had to know something. His face was ashen and his hands began to shake as her mother took the tea cup from him and rested it on the table.

'I inadvertently dug up something in the garden,' she said hesitantly. 'It'll sort itself out though,' she promised. So much for her plan of asking their advice, she thought, mentally reminding herself not to bring up the subject again.

'Dad?' He looked at her as if he hadn't seen her. 'Dad, are you all right?'

'He's fine dear,' her mother said, quickly composing herself. 'Just a silly turn, that's all. Happens to the best of us I'm afraid. We all have to get old one day. So, it's all ok then is it?' her nervous squeak was tuneless as Sophie stuck a smile on her face.

'Its ok, Dad,' she said, 'it's almost over now. I promise.'

'What else did Gran leave for you then?' her father asked after tea as they admired the garden. Sophie surveyed him carefully before answering. His eyes were more alert than earlier. The colour had returned gradually as her mother plied him with more tea. She suspected he had slipped in some brandy or something but she wasn't going to ask. So far so safe she thought. Here goes.

'Just a little money that's all,' she answered, admiring the garden. It was certainly going to look beautiful for the summer, which was more than she could say for hers. 'Didn't she leave you anything at all?' she asked for the hundredth time. Her father shook his head, returning to his raking of the leaves across the perfect lawn. The silence was comforting in a way, she wanted to offer them money but the fear of humiliating them was too much to contemplate. How else could she do it, just send them a cheque at Christmas or something...there had to be a way around it. It wasn't right that she had everything.

'Dad,' she ventured, breaking into his daydream. 'You know what I dug up in the garden don't you?'

'I've an idea,' he said still raking the leaves. 'Your Gran wanted you to have the house, so you can stop feeling guilty about that, I always knew it would bypass me. She did tell me you know,' he pointed a finger at her and resumed the raking. Sophie nodded obediently. Clearly it didn't matter how old you got, you still obeyed your parents! Well, she did anyway.

'Ok Dad, I promise. How come you know anyway?'

'About the house or the skeletons in your garden?' Sophie shot him a surprised smirk and he laughed lightly. 'Your Gran suspected a long while ago,' he said, 'she mentioned something to me one day. I swore I thought she was going senile bless her. Seems she may have been right. I've no idea how she knew though.' The leaves were now tidily stacked in a little heap.

'Who do you think those bones belonged to?' She watched his muscles freeze up. Stiffness encased him as he swept the small leaf pile into the larger heap he had already gathered. 'The police asked me to provide a list of the previous owners,' she rustled into her handbag and pulled out a duplicate she had made of the list. Her father took it and read down it slowly.

'That patio hasn't always been there my love,' he said, his voice flat and cold as he handed the list back to her. 'To tell you the truth I think they are human remains.' Sophie took note of his stern look, the fatherly *leave it be* look that she had been treated to as a little girl. 'But I can't be sure; and I don't want to cloud your view. My mum was lovely but she didn't live there that long. Chances are it goes back to my grandfather's brother or his family line. I didn't see much of my great uncle and aunt when they were alive and they've long since died I'm afraid,' he smiled at her gently and she knew the moment had now passed. 'Let the police carry on, it's their job to sort it all out, not ours.' Sophie knew there was no point in pursuing the conversation. Her father had said his piece and that was all. She would get nothing further from him now.

It was abundantly evident that the mobile stage was not going to be an easy task. *You'll pick it up won't you dear* the headmaster had said and strolled off as if collecting a large portable stage singled handed was the simplest thing in the world.

'Thank you again so much…for…for…helping me…with this,' Sophie breathed heavily as she heaved one end of the large wooden stage up into the air.

'Anytime,' Andy called back, his voice drifting up and over the stage pieces, his body hidden from sight.

The stage consisted of four rectangle boxes, each having one side cut out to allow a hollow base to form beneath the players. The connecting links had to be applied between the rear two boxes first. The front two slotted into the rear two.

Unleashing the boxes from one another had been simple but moving them was turning out to be much more of a challenge. At least for her, Andy seemed to be shifting them about as if there were made of air.

'Here,' she heard him say, 'just stay still and I'll take that from you.' She obeyed, her breath too short to speak. Being single Sophie had juggled numerous bags of shopping all by herself before, moved into the house alone, nearly broke her back with boxes full of books, shuffled washing machines and fridge freezers around the rooms and danced the settee into place, but nothing had prepared her for the sheer weight of these wooden boxes.

A loud bang echoed around the empty community hall like a gong and Sophie jumped, the wooden box grasped in her hands flimsily falling like a rock. Another gong. Above the echoing and the ringing in her ears she heard Andy chuckling and eventually saw him half way down the hall, the box planted firmly back on the floor and Andy himself giggling like a child. She smiled at him and began to laugh at the sight of him; his lean fit body bent into spasms of uncontrollable laughter.

'Why....why didn't they send a team...to help you?' Andy managed between chuckles. Sophie was too busy laughing herself now to answer. The stage lay in four pieces across the floor of the hall. After half an hour they had only managed to unhook each piece from the others and now they faced the task of moving them into the trailer that Andy had hooked up to his van. It was ludicrously tricky, especially seeing as they couldn't seem to manage to exit the hall with a piece at a time!

'Right, ok,' Andy mastered control again, 'lets take this piece out together – do you think you can lift one end?' Sophie nodded amidst giggles and joined him at the fallen piece. 'Ok, here goes nothing,' he said, 'we lift on three.' She nodded and clutched onto the edges of the wooden box as best she could. 'One, two, two and a half...'

'Get on with it you silly sod!' she cried, 'three,' and began to ease her side off the ground. Andy beamed back at her over the scratched wooden surface and they shuffled towards the open double doors of the hall, side-stepping until they made it outside to the trailer.

'Ok, so, you lower your end into the trailer and I'll take the weight,' he instructed.

'Like this?' she queried, glad to be losing the weight at last and wishing she had demanded a pay rise for the undertaking of this momentous task.

'Yeah, slowly does it,' he called, 'that's it, good.' Andy began to push his end up until the wooden box stood by itself vertically. He rubbed his hands together to loosen the dust. Sophie watched almost mesmerised as he wiped his hands down his thighs. She was glad Linda had told her the bad news in a way, at least now before she had made a complete idiot of herself. The fact that he already had a wife didn't stop her wanting to rip his clothes off and have hot passionate sex right there in the community hall though.

'Sophie?'

She flinched guiltily and shook her hair forwards to cover her blush. Now she knew that particular pleasure was never going to happen she felt suddenly more at ease around him – until he caught her in the midst of her favourite day dream.

'Shall we?' he chirped happily, 'just another three to go!'

'Yes, yes, of course,' she hurried inside before he could see her new scarlet shade. It was becoming a permanent feature, she really had to learn to control it, or get him out her life. He was the root cause of her blushing after all. Funny thing was though, even though she knew she couldn't have him to herself, she didn't want him to exit her life, but could she really settle for friends?

They worked furiously to load the other three pieces in exactly the same fashion. As Sophie locked up the hall and hid the keys in her jeans pocket Andy tied the boxes together with straps, thick cord entwined them at his expert hand and secured them to the base of the trailer. Moments later they were pulling into the school playground ready for phrase two – the unloading.

'So, do you think we got to take this back or will the community hall manager pick it up? Andy asked from behind one of the stage pieces.

'I've no idea actually, the headmaster arranged it, not very well admittedly,' she told him pushing the wooden lump as hard as she could along the school hall's polished floor and praying it wouldn't mark. 'Worse case scenario I'll have to do this all again!'

'Can't wait!' Andy laughed, 'give me a ring,' he offered. 'In for a penny, in for a pound,' he said as the wooden box lowered to the ground with ease under his expert skill, revealing him to her once more. With a thud Sophie's box hit the ground and she leapt back to mind her toes. She wiped her forehead with her arm and smiled at him across the stage. His bright eyes looked at her; his weight foremost on one leg. 'You ok?' he asked quietly.

'Yeah, thanks,' she said. 'Really, I mean it. I don't know what I'd have done without you. Can I, um, can I buy you a drink?' she coloured slightly willing it to fade fast. 'I mean to say thank you, of course,' the words tumbled freely.

'Yeah ok, but only if you let me pay,' he grinned broadly. 'Come on, let's get out of here.'

The sensation hit her the moment Andy swung open one of the double doors and the music flooded out like a wave. *Sweet Child O'Mine* blasted from the massive speakers by the door as Sophie and Andy headed towards a vacant table at the far side of the pub.

'This is my favourite place,' Andy called over the music. 'It'll be quieter over there,' he gestured towards the table in the corner and Sophie led the way. This was not part of the plan she thought, chastising her poor attempt at resistance. She had promised herself faithfully she would not spend any more time than necessary with Andy, since the horrid discovery that he had a wife already. The words had fallen from her moist lips quite surprisingly, even to her. Disengaged brain, she decided, *put it back into gear* she told herself sharply. *Do it now.*

'What would you like?'

'I'll have a small white wine please,' she said, rolling her coat into the corner and sliding across the padded seat against the wall. Andy removed his coat and hung it over the chair opposite her. 'Be right back,' he smiled.

Sophie watched him standing at the bar, his elbows leaning comfortably on the high bar surface as he waited patiently for the over-stretched barman to take his order. The pub was crowded, largely due to the live band, but the atmosphere was warm and inviting and Sophie felt herself relax into the seat. Surely it was ok to be friends with the man she thought, so long as she controlled herself. It wasn't as if they were having a hot affair amidst the paint tins, splashes of paint revealingly plastering the walls at will, the brushes strewn chaotically around the floor...

'Here you are,' he said, resting a lean glass in front of her. Sophie jolted up and smiled quickly.

'Sorry – day dreaming – I do it all the time,' she confessed shyly. 'Bad habit. Thank you,' she said indicating the glass. Andy took his seat and held a pint of bitter to the air.

'Cheers,' he laughed 'to amateur dramatics.'

'Cheers,' she clinked her glass gently against his. 'Will you be coming to the fete?'

'Oh yeah, my Annabel will be in it,' he beamed proudly. 'Last weekend she told me she wanted to be an actress so I have to go, it'll be the dog house for me if I miss it, not that I would.'

The music had moved on from rock to a modern song that Sophie knew but couldn't tell you the artist if her life were staked on it. Several people were bopping around the makeshift dance area where three of the tables had been cleared for the band. It was quieter now and Sophie took a sip of her wine, gratefully.

'What's the play going to be?' Andy asked.

'I found it on the religious education syllabus,' she said. 'Can't remember its name but it basically teaches the lesson of Easter and the resurrection of Christ. It's all about the meaning of Easter eggs, how they represent the new life of the baby chicks just like the new life of Jesus when he rose from the dead. It's a bit serious I suppose, but no more so than the nativity at Christmas. Last year it was a real success but we've never had an Easter theme at a summer fete before. I can't imagine what my head master was thinking.'

Charlotte Church sang *Crazy Chick* from the pub's surround-sound system as the band began to dismantle their instruments all over the floor. Wires trailed the floor like a maze.

'If it goes well he'll probably want the same every year,' Andy mused. 'Guess I'd better start scheduling that stage removal into my diary,' he smiled. 'There was something I wanted to ask you,' he said, taking a long sip of bitter. Sophie inclined her head to the right. 'Do you think you could, I mean, would you mind writing a reference for me. It's for another client, they won't commission me without one and I don't actually have any. Most people just say thanks and call me again in a year or two. Only if it's not too much trouble.'

'I don't see why not,' she smiled. 'I'll make a start on it tonight. Is there anything specific you want me to include?'

'No, no just whatever you think. I should have waited to ask you until we'd finished your place really, but well, you can wait to write it if you want.'

'Don't be silly,' she said feeling a flush of confidence. 'I'm sure you'll finish it just as well as you've started. I'll write it later. After I've marked the homework,' she sighed.

'Thank you, I sort of knew I could count on you.' A deep silence lay between them. Andy's eyes smiled around the corners. He coughed lightly and drew back in his chair, took another large sip of bitter. 'Annabel doesn't get that much homework,' he said. Sophie sipped her wine quietly. What had happened there? It wasn't dissimilar to the kitchen the other day. Why were all the nice ones married? Life simply wasn't fair. Unless she was very much mistaken he was just as attracted to her as she was to him.

'No,' she answered, remembering he had spoken. It was far too easy to gaze at him happily. 'It doesn't really kick in until secondary school but the habit is sort of set in place early these days. It won't take me long exactly; it's only a picture of their families at Easter time. We're having an Easter egg hunt at the fete and the pictures will be on display so we've got to get them drawn ready.'

'Yeah, I think I remember hearing about a picture of an Easter egg. She was making those chocolate shreddie things with her mother the other day, you know the ones where you put a Cadbury's mini egg in and it looks like the birds nest?'

Sophie laughed nervously at the mention of Annabel's mother.

'Yes, I know them all too well. Try making hundred's every year and you won't forget them as long as you live,' she smiled.

'Bit odd isn't it? I mean having an Easter egg hunt in the middle of summer.'

'Our headmaster is a bit odd,' Sophie smiled at his chuckle. 'Anyway, it's a chocolate hunt really but the kids had so many nice Easter egg pictures on the walls that some of them are being put out to mark the spots as it were.'

'So it's not really about Easter then?'

'Not really, just utilising what we've got from last term. I admit the play is a bit daft but as I said, our headmaster is a little odd,' she laughed.

The pub thinned out once the band had gone but Sophie didn't notice. The noise level dropped significantly and the clock ticked on. They chatted easily for what felt like an hour, each leaning forward on the table, close enough to touch.

Outside the sun was setting, casting a beam to spread across their table like a blessing. Sophie felt warm and happy. She pushed all thoughts away from her mind, except him. This was her time, she was behaving herself, only just, but she was.

'We should really come here again,' he said, 'the food is excellent' he told her. She nodded in agreement. Eventually Andy offered to take her home and she accepted graciously.

The alarm clock startled her. Sophie squinted her eyes closed tighter and wished it wasn't time to get up. She switched off the alarm and lay in the stillness for a moment. What had she let herself in for? Heartache. Good old simple, heartache. The sensation she felt on entering the pub was the same one that kept her warm all through her cosy chat with Andy, all through the journey home and the same one that held her wrapped up in her dream all night long. It was the sensation of being in love. All right, it had been years, but she hadn't forgotten what it felt like and she knew all too well that was what it boiled down to. Furthermore, despite the problem of his being married, she couldn't shake it off. It was already too late.

Reluctantly she dragged herself out of the encapsulating warmth of the bedcovers and stood under the shower, the water smothering her highly charged body. It was going to be a long day she decided.

Sophie sat quietly at the desk as the children fled the room noisily. The screen behind her gave away the day's activities to anyone viewing it. She signed off the laptop and the screen flashed into darkness.

Literacy and early numbers before and after the morning break followed by literacy hour in the afternoon class. They had finished with reading and now the children charged out towards weary looking parents, their boundless energy a constant mystery to Sophie. But the day was far from over. The after-school activities were only just beginning and today marked the first rehearsal of the fete's dramatics. She smiled at the memory of her and Andy moving the mobile stage into the hall. It was about to make its début.

The great hall was not so great; in fact it was quite small now that the mobile stage took up a significant portion. Still, the headmaster had wanted a stage and he certainly had one.

'Right, children, quiet please,' she called in her most assertive voice. The girls and boys gathered around her, a sea of grey trousers and skirts with navy blue cardigans and jumpers. Their expectant eyes looked up at her quizzically. Angels, she thought, innocent angels until the moment they opened their mouths!

'We are going to have a fete, and that means we're going to have a play too. Now, because you all made such lovely things about Easter recently we're going to use some of them at the fete.'

'What about the chocolate hunt miss?' A chorus of yeses' and excited cries mounted.

'Shss, the chocolate hunt too, yes, it'll be after the play. Now,' she commanded, 'silence please while I explain this play to you. Now, because we're going to use your artwork about your Easter holidays we thought we would have a play about Easter too. Who knows what Easter is all about and I don't mean chocolate eggs. Anyone?'

'Is it about Jesus Miss?' a tiny voice asked.

'No, silly it's about God,' the boy next to her argued.

'Quiet!' Sophie said, 'you're both right. I'll explain. Jesus died on the cross, you remember that from your lessons yesterday with Mr Pagent?' A sea of heads bobbed in understanding, or union, sometimes it was hard to tell. 'Well, God sacrificed his son, Jesus, so that we may all have life today. But Jesus came back to life, remember, and Easter is about celebrating his return to life. So, who wants to be in the play?'

The chorus 'I do Miss, I do Miss, I do,' filled the room, echoing up to the high ceiling and sounding far louder than reality.

Sophie quietened them down as best she could and stepped up onto the stage. The children had been perched on the edge and now stood to climb up too.

'We need five of you to read the lines. Everyone else will be in the choir. Who wants to read?'

'Right ok, Annabel, you can read child number 1, here you go,' she handed the pretty little girl a sheet of words typed boldly in large font. Annabel took them happily. 'Now, you can stand over here. Yes, Jimmy, you can read child number 2, here you are, Peter you can be child number 3, Lucy child number 4 and Lisa child number 5. Right, stand in a line next to Annabel, that's right. The rest of you, gather behind them. Mr Ingles will be here in a minute to teach you the song you're going to sing.'

'Postman Pat, postman pat, postman pat and his black and white cat...' Jimmy began to sing and the children roared with laugher.

'Quiet!' Sophie screamed. 'Jimmy if you sing that again you're be relegated to the choir and you won't be allowed to read those lines. Do I make myself clear?'

'Yes Miss,' a small voice amidst the deathly silence.

'Good, right, ah here comes Mr Ingles. Hello Pat,' she said quietly as the music teacher arrived. 'Right children, Mr Ingles will teach you the song.' Pat smiled at her and she tried not to laugh. He seemed oblivious to the children's mocking of him. Just as well she thought.

'Now, let's get started. First you four make sounds as if you feel sick. Uuurgh, uurgh, and Annabel you start with your first line. Read it with me, the rest of you are now quiet and listen. *What's the matter with you?* Very good. Now, Jimmy, you read *I feel sick, really sick* and Lisa, Lucy and Peter, you all say *we've eaten too many Easter eggs*. Very good, now Annabel you say...' Sophie waited for the girl to read the line.

'No won...'

'Yes, that's wonder,' she prompted.

'No wonder you feel sick,'

'Good, now you four make those sounds again, very good. Now Annabel, your next line...'

'Well it serves...?' she looked up.

'Yes, that's right, go on.'

'...serves you all right then. I bet you don't know what Easter eggs mean do you?'

'Well done Annabel, that's very very good. Now Jimmy, your line, read with me *go on them tell us what Easter eggs mean.*'

The children progressed slowly through the five minute reading, taking the entire hour to complete all the lines but Sophie was glad she had got them through the whole thing. It had been easier than she thought. She had picked the best readers from the bunch. The short reading was a simple explanation of what Easter represented. Annabel went on to tell the others that the egg represented the unborn chick and the chick represented new life, and that was what Easter was all about. Should be simple she convinced herself as she climbed into her car and headed home. Should be simple. In the background the choir had began, badly sounding a rendition of something she had never heard of, or worse still it was meant to be something she had actually heard of...oh well, that was postman pat's job.

The roads were fairly quiet thankfully and she pulled into her driveway in a matter of minutes, glad to be home finally. She had successfully shoved Andy out of her mind every few minutes he popped into it and now faced an empty evening, which was going to be more challenging not to think about him. The decorating was due to commence again tomorrow night.

As she walked in through her front door, grateful beyond all reason that the day was finally done, she almost trod on it. Her heart froze. It couldn't be... Shakily she opened the envelope.

I'M BORED. PERHAPS I SHOULD KILL YOU. MAYBE THAT WOULD FILL UP A FEW POINTLESS HOURS. YOU COULD REST WITH ELISE, AND HER LOVER BOY. YOU'D LIKE THAT WOULDN'T YOU.

I'LL HAVE TO THINK ABOUT IT, THERE MAY BE SOMETHING EVEN MORE EXCITING I COULD DO WITH YOU. WAIT AND SEE!

A lump grew in her throat and she realised she was going to have to go to the police. Whatever had she done to deserve this?

Chapter Six

Today Frederick bought me a gift. This is an unusual event and I am curious as to what prompted him to act in such a way. He must want something. Isn't it horrible how pessimistic I have become. That is not a question but a fact. He has bought me a watch. Sadly for Frederick he still doesn't know me very well. A watch will only remind me of how much time is passing me by. After twenty-one years of marriage he still doesn't know what I really need from him.

The mystery as to why he has bought it remains unclear. I wonder if he has been unfaithful and now suffers from guilt...

I sit by my window remembering when we first met. It was romantic. It was wonderful. I thought I had died and been re-born into a new life, one that couldn't possibly be mine. I kept pinching the skin on the back of my hand to make sure I was alive. To make sure I wasn't dreaming.

It was a warm day in September in 1913, about four o'clock in the afternoon. I had just finished work and left the shop. My boss was locking up. I had to find somewhere to live in a few months. The foster care arrangement was due to come to an end and I would be on my own.

Frederick was standing across the street attempting to hail a taxicab. He stood near to my bus stop. I walked towards the bus stop and stood by the board. As usual I was the only one being picked up at this time of day. Frederick smiled at me and came to stand by my side.

'Hello,' he said in a deep voice. I noticed he was quite short as I stood beside him.

'Hello,' I said, my own voice sounding distant to me. Had I even spoken out loud? I watched his face for a reaction. He had dark hair, which crept down his face by his ears and framed his face to perfection.

'Do you know if this bus is usually on time?' he asked me.

'No, it's usually quite late,' I replied. His eyes were dark too. I watched his pupils dilate as he smiled at me again. The sun moved casually behind a cloud as if to give us privacy.

'Oh,' he said. 'Do you catch it often?'

'Yes, every day when I finish work' I said. 'Over there,' I pointed to the shop where my boss was just depositing the keys in her handbag and walking away.

'My name's Fred,' he said, extending his hand. 'Short for Frederick.' He coughed slightly and I shook his hand. 'Harris. Frederick Harris.'

'I'm pleased to make your acquaintance Mr Harris. I'm Elise Trent.' He smiled at me, his white teeth in a perfect row. I smiled back shyly.

'I cannot seem to attract a taxicab. Would you mind if I wait here with you?'

'Not at all Sir,' I replied.

'Thank you. It would be a novelty indeed to take a bus. Yes,' he seemed to be warming to the idea, 'I'll take the bus, why not!'

We stood in silence for a while, the bus nowhere to be seen. Frederick wore a smart black suit and hat. It was apparent from the start that he was a gentleman – a wealthy gentleman at that. I remember feeling quite pathetically attired next to him and prayed the bus would arrive so we could take our polite parting. Surely he would not sit next to me. The bus was usually quite empty at this time of day. It was not that he was unattractive but merely that I was so far from his apparent circles of life that I hadn't the faintest idea what to say to him.

'Tell me, Elise, would you be kind enough to accompany me to the theatre on Saturday?' he spoke quite suddenly.

'There is a new Shakespeare production and I was thinking of going to see it.'

I remember how I felt, dizzy, my heart bounding up and down and my face flushed crimson. Surely this gentleman, this man of obvious class wasn't asking for my company...? He must be mistaken. I looked around, there was nobody else present. He had to have been talking to me then...This was a new life and by some luck it was actually mine.

'Thank you Sir, I would be happy to,' I answered, my voice shaky with nerves.

'Excellent, I shall collect you in my carriage. Pray, tell me, where do you reside?'

'I'm orphaned,' I told him quietly, feeling the near dream slipping away. 'I live at the home on Tennyson Avenue,' to which he half smiled at me. 'But only for a few weeks then I'll be leaving,' I added a little too quickly.

'Oh really, evicting you out are they?' his mouth twisted into a grin.

'Well, yes Sir, actually they are. I have to find somewhere quite soon. You see they have to make space. New children arrive almost daily. It's very crowded.' His face was puzzled and I bit my tongue. Was I putting him off me so soon?

'I am positive we can find you somewhere nice. I'll help you look,' he volunteered. I beamed back at him.

'You are too kind Sir,' I replied. The bus began to blur into view from further up the road. Deciding against the bus after all Frederick took his leave. He bowed gallantly.

'I look forward to the pleasure of your company on Saturday Miss Trent,' he replaced his hat and sauntered away.

When I boarded the bus we overtook him strolling along the pathway and he lifted his hat to me.

That was that. Quite simple. Today I think about how ludicrous it all was, how easily I was impressed and impressed by what exactly? I was naïve, young, unguided and alone. Excuses? I prefer to think of them as reasons for why I acted the way I did. Still, ludicrous it was and ludicrous it remains to this day.

We sat in the back row of the theatre. I didn't like the play much, but then I didn't see that much of it. About five minutes in Fred yawned, his arm stretching above his head. When I think back now this was typical stuff, nothing fancy, but it felt wonderful then. His hand fell to rest across the back of my seat. We were nestled into the chairs. The couples either side had as little room as us. About ten minutes into the production I was already getting bored of the bronzed superstar who felt it his duty to leap over every stage prop and swoon at a dozen people at each turn. Fred turned towards me, his gaze fiercely penetrating. My heart skipped as his fingers played along my arm. This was very forward behaviour in its day. When I think about it now it was a shade less than civil. I think with interest now how much his mother would have berated me for such abandonment of class!

Then, as if he couldn't take it any more, he lunged towards me and I found myself clumsily locked into his embrace.

I don't think I looked up again until the audience's applause drowned all other noise. If anybody in the theatre actually watched the play I would be surprised. It was filled with young people no older than us. A sea of heads turning one way or another. Partly I felt sorry for the actors. They were trying their best. It must have been very disconcerting to realise that their audience were not interested in their performance in the least.

'Good play wasn't it,' he smiled as we left with the mob through the front doors. I laughed at him lightly and agreed that it was most exciting. He took my arm and we walked along the road slowly.

'Did you have education Miss Trent,' he asked me. 'I am thinking perhaps a governess?'

'Yes, a governess, she was very well educated. She taught quite a few of us at the home, all together. When I was older I attended the local school for a short while. And you Sir?'

'I hated school,' he said shortly. 'I was enormously glad to leave.' It was then that I saw the look of evil in his eyes for the first time. It's a look as hard as diamonds, stern and unforgiving. I didn't recognise it for what it was back then. I didn't realise it would stay with him forever. If I had known perhaps I would have thought more carefully. But then, I was up against a time line. I had to find somewhere to live and here he was, a possible future right in front of me; a gentleman paying me, a mere orphan, his attention. It hardly seemed likely to last but one never knew. It did happen, one read of such connections in the national newspapers, their families either displeased by them publicly and making a great show of cutting them off without an inheritance or hushing up one of the party's background.

'Why?' My face must have looked so innocent. He smirked at me quickly, rolling his eyes back and giving a twisted laugh.

'The people. Children. I hated them all. Children are terrible creatures. I thank God we don't stay that way forever, but you will forgive me my dear Elise, I run away with my feelings on the subject.'

I should have known, I should have backed off right then. But I didn't.

'Some children are well behaved,' I venture. 'There are some who have had most unfortunate backgrounds and they manage to lead highly satisfactory lives, eventually.'

'Yes of course, I imagine so,' he tried to be brighter. 'I found school life very challenging. There are always those who are unpleasant to one of breeding. You have not had the misfortune to mix with the lower classes Miss Trent. They are savages, let me tell you, I shall endeavour not to allow them the pleasure of your privileged company.' There was an awkward silence. He let my hand go and began to quicken his pace. 'May I walk you home or would you prefer that I summon a taxi? I know there are many carriages close by if you should feel too faint to make the journey by foot. Pray tell me, what does my lady desire?'

I had never heard such language, such grandeur, to be treated in such a way!

If I only knew it these would be the best days of our lives together. Just a short few months into the new year of 1914 and Frederick would be called up to the front line. Minutes before he left the country we would be married and I would be stuck with the man whose already slightly misty personality had been irrevocably darkened, his mind poisoned by the traumas of war and his temper beyond all reasonable control.

If only I had mustered the common sense to realise his family would never sanction such a match, or if they did would torture me mercilessly forever. His father was to die in the great war leaving his mother a widow, consequently a permanent resident in our home.

Life is not like those magical first few weeks anymore. I cannot recall the last time we went to the cinema, or the last time we went anywhere together. He goes out to his club of course, daily, and for long spells at a time. I, on the other hand, am waiting for him. Always waiting. A friend once told me that so long as he thinks I am there, waiting, he won't hurry home. Maybe they are right, it certainly seems to be proving to be the case. Frederick is out at the minute. I suspect he will stay out for a while yet. It has only been a mere three hours, four hours is the bare minimum so far as I have surmised. It can easily be longer than that.

When he comes in he will dress for dinner. We will sit at the dinner table and I will pretend not to notice his state of intoxication. We eat at eight every evening and the meal will be in the best possible state it can be preserved in the event that he is late, or fallen asleep whilst dressing. He will eat, greedily, obliging his mother's persistent need for conversation with the confirmative nod or word of absolute agreement. Neither my husband nor mother-in law will barely register my presence. He will sit listening to the wireless at top volume, his choice of programme – always his choice. Then after about thirty minutes his head will start to rock softly on his hand that supports it. He will continue to jolt himself back into consciousness until the snoring kicks in; at which point I will subtly make moves towards the stairs – in hopes to hint that bed wouldn't be such a bad idea as he can barely keep his eyes open. Throughout this scene his mother will embroider her tapestries. She will sit bolt upright and insist I do the same.

"Sit up straight girl!" she will roar. I will do so for fear of further chastisement. It seems not to matter to her that her son is slouched like a wet weekend across three quarters of the long seat.

In time Frederick will see the sense in my suggestion and my instruction to "go up" will be declared. I am never afraid of the night. He doesn't want much in that area these days, particularly as he falls asleep the split second his head hits the pillow. Then I am free to dream.

This world of forbidden acts, forbidden people and forbidden imaginary lives is completely open to me and in my mind's eye I am running towards it with more energy than I know how to experience. Suddenly I recall Mrs Betty and her insistent pursuit of tracking down Freud's *Interpretation of Dreams*. Sadly Mrs Betty was doomed to be disappointed and could never find a copy of the much talked about book. Dreams are a freedom, whoever you are and whatever your life is like. I take pleasure in this freedom.

7th March 1935– Diary of Elise Harris

It occurs to me now that when I accepted it was more out of desperation than admiration for him. Me; the most romantic fool there ever was, married for the worst possible reason; because it seemed the best option at the time. How I've changed, how much I've grown up since that day. Then I was a naïve nineteen year old who thought that marriage to Frederick Harris was the only life available. If I knew then what I know now maybe things would have turned out differently... How many people have said that? Regrets are such terrible things. They haunt you like nightmares. The guilt sweeps over me every time I wonder why it is he wasn't shot down in the war to end all wars. It didn't end my war, the little emotional battle that I had to fight day after day. His dark moods, his violent temper... the list is endless.

I have wondered if I could just run away from him, to leave his morbid schedule of dull routine and vanish into thin air. I have attempted to break into the desk and to swiftly digest the figures from the bank statements into my memory but so far have not succeeded. He keeps his desk draw locked and without smashing the thing I cannot access it. The key doesn't leave his person. I begin to hatch a plan to steal it whilst he sleeps and make a copy. I begin to frighten myself of the repercussions of this plan if I am caught in the act. I begin to get scared.

How have I managed to end up in this situation? Marrying him was such a stupid move. I recall it again, despite the fact I'd rather forget the entire episode.

It was a bright August day in 1914. We had gone for a walk in the park, eaten ice-cream and were sitting on a park bench watching the ducks on the pond, and the children playing, their parents running after them like headless chickens.

Frederick shuffled on the bench, always striving to look taller than his five foot six frame. Unfortunately for Frederick he was never going to grow the extra two inches it would take to level with me. He was yet to discover an alternative method of being the biggest influence in our future household.

I smiled at him, all too familiar with his shuffling and finding it faintly amusing. He half chuckled as he straightened his back to achieve that extra inch in his eyes. We sat quietly on the bench, the sun on our backs and the scene unfolding before us. The scene of the future, our future, I hoped. The little children playing harmlessly, driving their parents to distraction, complete innocence.

I caught him watching me, his dark eyes piercing. His smile crept slowly across his face. It was at that very moment that I noticed his hair, dashing almost, a style more befitting to the previous century but charming in its own unique way.

'Would you like children one day?' I asked him. His smile tightened at the words. I watched his face with interest.

'Maybe, one day,' he said his voice quite flat, as was its custom. I turned back to the scene before us just in time to catch one child giggle at her fathers tickling. I smiled at them and then back at Frederick. He was still watching me.

'What?' I laughed at him. He put his arms around me, drew me closer and we sat for a while watching the families in the park.

It was when we were walking back that he stopped suddenly. I stopped two steps ahead of him. Swiftly he caught up with me and stood in front of me. He looked different, a concentrated frown taking over his facial muscles.

'What's wrong?' I whispered, fearing some sudden jolt of pins and needles or something similar.

'Elise dear, I have a question for you. Here, take a seat here,' he said indicating the handily placed bench by the bus stop.

I sat, as instructed. He knelt on the ground, produced a small velvet box from his jacket pocket. I stared at him, stunned into silence.

'Elise my dear, as you know I've been called up to the front line this month. I depart tomorrow.' His voice was confident despite the topic it covered. I pleaded with him to waver the subject, closing my eyes and sighing deeply. I didn't want to think about it. He clasped my hands in his. 'Look at me Elise, look at me.' I did as obeyed. His voice was harder this time, more assertive. 'I need to have you waiting for me, I need to know I've got something to fight for, something to come home to.' He held my gaze a moment that felt like an eternity. 'Elise, will you do me the honour of consenting to be my wife?'

After what felt like forever I managed to string together a sort of mumble and nodded my head. He pulled me into his shirt and I stayed there, muffled and in the dark.

We were married at the local registry office, his troops waiting outside for him to join them in the army truck. The moment after we'd shared our first kiss as a married couple he turned to me, 'Elise, I have to go to battle. Go to my mother. She will have great need of you now that I am gone.' And he was gone. I watched the truck drive away, waving my bouquet in the air. I'd never felt so alone, not even on the steps of the children's home.

It would be easier if I could hate him but putting aside his strops he hasn't actually done anything wrong. I'm just not in love with him. Life would be so much simpler if I were.

18th October 1935 - Diary of Elise Harris

I am thirty eight years old now. Sometimes I wonder if life will ever change or if this is exactly how it will remain for the rest of my days.

Today Clarissa was worse than ever. She behaves like an over-indulgent child and I cannot understand why. She has always had money, has never been short of food, water, shelter, love. Well, love is debatable. I am not at all convinced that she knows what love is. She has never been abandoned, does not know what it feels like to be left completely alone in the world.

"I want pork, girl," she demanded at dinner this evening. "I expressly told you I wanted pork tonight and you coldly serve me beef." At this point poor Betsy attempted to explain that the butcher was fresh out of pork. "Kindly do not interrupt me when I am lecturing you child. Now pay attention, you will remove this carcass from my table." Betsy stood silently. "Now! Now I say," she bellowed and Betsy removed the plate. "I am not finished! You will stand there and listen to me," she admonished the frightened Betsy who had considered it time to take her leave of the dining room. "I have said it before and I will say it again. It is as well for a girl to become aware of her shortcomings early in life. Your shortcoming child is not to pay attention. You WILL pay attention to me when I am speaking to you. Is that quite clear?" Betsy opened her mouth to speak and lamely closed it again. "I should think so and close your mouth child. Do not stand there like that. Go, take this monstrous meal away and bring me pork." Betsy scuttled away quickly. Through this episode I remained quiet, feeling terrible for Betsy but knew only too well there was nothing I could do for her whilst Clarissa was in full flow.

"It is quite true Mrs Harrris," I attempted meekly. "For I heard it myself from Mrs Meyers that pork is quite unavailable at the present."

"Do be quiet girl," was all the response I was to receive. Thankful in some small way that I too wasn't going to receive a repeat of the lecture.

"Really they should try to appease mother's wishes," Frederick agreed. "I mean how difficult can it be to serve a meal. Really, one cannot find good staff these days," Frederick mused.

"Um, yes. Frederick," Clarissa commanded. "You will take me out to dine this evening. They have excellent pork at the Pump rooms. Come boy, come," she rose nosily from her seat; her ruffles of maroon fabric dress around her like a shield. The black choker about her neck stretched with the attempt of her voice to outshine any other sound in the room and her pearls bounced lightly against her wrinkled skin. The lace trim of her dress cost more than my annual clothing allowance. Despite being one of the wealthiest families in the town my mother-in-law does not see fit to bestow any of *her family's* money on an outsider. Being without connections I will always be an outsider, Frederick's wife or not.

Clarissa stood, her chin to the ceiling, waiting for her son to take her arm. Her greying hair is always bound up in a tight knot on top of her head like a crown. I sometimes wonder if she were to let it down, how long it would be. The style, she once told me during one of her rare pleasanter moments, is modelled on the late Queen Victoria.

"Good evening Mrs Harris," she addressed me as they left the room. "I am sure that girl can find you some nourishment. Goodness knows I afford her an ample housekeeping allowance for groceries." As they departed I could distinctly hear her shrill tones. "I shall despatch a telegram to my sister Mrs Gregson tomorrow Frederick. I shall make enquires into her own pork supplies. If they are able to obtain pork I fail to see why we cannot…"

89

So it was that I returned to the kitchen and Betsy re-served the beef to me in the dining room.

"Mrs Harris and Mr Harris have gone out for the evening," I explained to Betsy. "If there is any of the beef left I would be grateful if you could…"

"Yes of course Madam," Betsy, a most obliging girl in my experience, "right away Madam."

1ˢᵗ May 1935 – Diary of Elise Harris

Today something wonderful happened. I am so happy that I cannot bring myself to write coherently!

The devil himself has entered my soul I think. But he brings with him only joy. I should avoid all temptation but I find myself weak. I find I cannot think of anything but the possibility. What a possibility indeed he brings! Was I not right to pray for a miracle? Have I not suffered sufficient heartbreak and desolate loneliness to deserve even the slightest moment of cherished hope?

For the first time since my night on the steps of the children's home I do not know what will happen tomorrow. The suspense is thrilling, the excitement bubbling over without control. I must refrain from showing my true feelings. Clarissa and Frederick must not witness my gaiety. I must be guarded if I am to enjoy even the smallest possible chance of happiness.

Mr Thomas Brody. What a name! His eyes are the colour of the deepest sea and his hair the sandiest blond. I have never seen such a gentleman; his body lean and fit, no sign of the round mid-life shape that my husband finds himself laden with.

Upon introduction outside the tea shop today he opened the door for me and purchased a pot of tea for two. His voice when he spoke! I have never heard a sweeter sound. Oh dear diary, I am so glad to fill you with happy thoughts.

I have pledged to meet with him again soon. Please pray God let it be tomorrow for I am overflowing with joy. How shall I conceal such emotions? How can I bear so much happiness?

Chapter Seven

April 2009

Having delivered the list of ex-owners for her house to the local police station Sophie felt bleak. The drive home along the narrow country road was long and winding. The car hopped over the bumpy road steadily, the dusk heavily setting down for the night. All colours were seeped out of the countryside around her, leaving a black and white image like a carbon drawing. She drove further into the image, her headlights the only reflective source of life ahead of her. She yawned repeatedly, now driving slowly through the puddles that resembled small lakes. Her mind switched to the evening meal. Her stomach begged her for strength as she reached the end of the twisting country road. Nearly back home she told herself, turning right at the junction. Almost on the home straight, she thought.

In her mind's eye she saw her garden, the moon sliding across the patchy grass like a satin sheet, the light bouncing off it like a stage show. Just about right she muttered to herself, a stage show all right. The tall trees that brought up the rear towered over the moonlit lawn like guards, protecting the secrets that lay below. At least they had until the pond idea had sprung into her mind.

She wondered just how long the skeletons would have remained undetected if she hadn't chosen that very spot to dig. It was perfect for it, right beside the patio, the rockery area to the edge where the path led from the front of the house. Ideal for water mains for a fountain…why on earth didn't whoever buried them bury them someplace else, like right in the middle where nobody would ever dig? She didn't understand any of it, much less the reasoning behind it all.

Something told her it was going to be a long night; that sleep would evade her even though she cried out for it. The darkness settled into the car like a fog as she took the last few roads that led into the town, turning the block and reaching Convent Avenue; the road of doom she thought gloomily. Would it ever brighten up?

The next morning was Saturday and Sophie knew she had to go shopping. Andy was due to arrive in the early afternoon. They had completed three bedrooms and were now onto the smallest bedroom at the back, then they would move onto the stairs and hallway and finally into the lounge. Hopefully by that stage the garden would be free to touch again. She was no longer sure she wanted a pond. The whole idea was somehow tainted. Maybe she would leave the garden until next year... that would mean she could invite Andy back into her life for a brief spell. It would be something pleasant to look forward to during the long dark winter nights.

Shifting into action she got herself together and headed to Tesco, idly roamed the aisles picking up things she wasn't sure she actually needed at all. *Pull yourself* together she told herself and half-heartedly dug in her handbag for the list she had made earlier in the week. Aimlessly she studied the list and looked up to locate the cleaning products. Her eye caught the fantastic rear physic of a tall man ahead of her. He was selecting potatoes and onions. She watched him happily preparing to smile brightly as he half turned towards her. Shock replaced her momentary pleasure and the numbness that transfixed her face also glued her feet to the floor as she attempted to drag them towards the next aisle as quickly as possible. She couldn't possibly be seen by Andy as she was. In the supermarket! She had on her worse possible attire and hadn't even bothered with her hair. The full glamorous image was to be prepared upon her return home, freshly in time for his arrival...

Thankfully he hadn't seen her but mercilessly she kept seeing him and finally resolved to select birthday cards for everyone she knew for the next decade until she could be sure he had completed his shopping and left.

Sophie swerved her wayward trolley towards the cards and stayed there. God must hate me today, she thought, as she saw him approaching from the far end. He still hadn't seen her and was now picking out a big teddy bear with a bright red bow around its neck. Her heart melted momentarily and she dropped her guard. Then he moved to the flowers and picked up a bunch of roses. Her feet stuck stubbornly to the floor again. She spied wine in his wire basket and her whole body felt spiked with the reality she had been trying to ignore. He wasn't single. He definitely wasn't single. It was Saturday and he was clearly buying things to impress a lady with that evening. That lady was not going to be her.

She headed back towards the vegetables, no longer caring if he saw her or not. It wasn't worth the heartache, it simply wasn't. It was too cruel. Ridiculously she felt as if she would cry and felt like abandoning her shopping completely. Pride alone kept her from doing so as she trudged on around the store in search for a gift for Linda. Her maternity leave would start soon and she wanted to get her something special. She had wanted to, now all she wanted was to go home to her half-painted house with its torn up garden and cry her heart out. *Get a grip* she told herself but today it wasn't working as it usually did.

Andy spread the paint efficiently across the small bedroom wall as if it were gliding effortlessly. Sophie was busy splurging it into a corner in moody silence. The radio was on, the weekend downloads chart was up to number ten but Sophie couldn't have told you the last song played if you paid her.

'Are you alright Sophie?'

'Fine,' she said shortly. 'I'm fine,' splurging more paint viciously into the same spot. Another large clump of paint flew at her chest and cling stubbornly to her previously white blouse knotted together at the front. The blue cami top beneath the blouse had, so far, dodged the paint artfully.

'Ok,' he said, his eyes scanning the room frantically. 'Can you make a start on the far wall do you think?' He watched her as she made to move. She was definitely not herself. Sophie got up silently, moved over to the back wall and began throwing the paint into splashes on the wall and merging them messily.

'You're sure you're ok?'

'I'm fine,' her voice through gritted teeth. 'Really.'

'Right, good,' he said. 'So, we're almost finished up here,' he tried again. 'Almost into the hallway and then we've got the tricky part – the stairs. Now, do you want to start the living room and finish with the stairs? I just thought that that way you'd have all rooms functional again.'

'Whatever you think,' she whispered, her voice barely audible.

Andy watched her carefully; pleased the paint was going on smoother finally. The letterbox snapped shut downstairs and Sophie froze, her breath held in sharply. Andy gave her a quizzical stare.

'Shall I get it for you?' he asked cautiously. Sophie's eyes were staring at the door like a laser beaming through the walls and down to the mat. She nodded numbly. Andy rested his paintbrush down and skipped down the stairs two at a time. Sophie could feel her pulse quickening with his bounding energy. Her heart was racing with the thought of another letter. It was too much. It was all too much.

A large dollop of paint fell heavily from the over-laden brush in her hand and clustered on the bare wooden floorboards like a tiny mountain.

'Just some bills I think,' Andy smiled as he re-entered the room, handed her the stack of brown business-like envelopes and took up his brush again. Sophie took a deep breath and sank to the floor, the post in her lap, and burst into tears.

'Oh my God,' he came to her side and began to cradle her in his arms. She tried to shove him away but he was too strong and eventually she caved. It was so nice to be held by him. It was so nice to break from feeling completely alone. 'Whatever's wrong sweetheart?' he asked, his voice soothing.

Despite the fear she felt her lips curve reluctantly into a half smile. *Sweetheart, if only...*

'It's...it's silly,' she sobbed. 'It's so silly really...I've been getting these letters...this horrible letters.'

'You mean you've had another one?'

'Yeah, there have been more since the one you saw,' she said, her voice more of a whisper as she choked on the words with sobs. Andy squeezed her tighter. His body felt warm and comforting and she allowed herself to cling to him for a moment longer.

'I hope you've taken them to the police?' he asked, lifting her chin with his little finger to force her to look at him. It felt nice, his hand on her face. Spellbound by her own pointless emotions she felt a little better.

'Yes of course,' she sobbed, 'the second one I took there. I feel like that's all I do, run to the police.'

Andy just nodded at her.

'Nothing can go right at the moment,' she whispered. 'Everything I want is already taken,' she waved her arms suggestively around her but Andy was lost in her embrace 'or a complete disaster.'

'I hope you're not including my handiwork in that!' he chuckled. She smiled at him. 'Now come on, let's finish this room and have a cup of tea,' he encouraged, lifted her to her feet and handed her the paintbrush. 'Nicely does it now,' he wavered his own brush at her and she smiled again.

'Ok,' she agreed taking the brush and concentrating on the wall. It was better than crying at any rate she decided. With all credibility blown to the wind she had nothing left to lose now. If she saw him in Tesco's again she would say hello she decided, even if she were dressed as if she were about to be condemned to labour camp.

Andy made her tea strong and placed it in front of her at the kitchen table. She smiled in thanks and gratefully took a sip. The dried paint on both their hands covered their mugs as

95

they sat in companionable silence. Her limbs ached like nothing she had experienced before. Surely, decorating wasn't supposed to be this exhausting. She considered asking him but despite recent events she felt she couldn't bear to part with the tiny shred of dignity she had left in tact.

'So did you decide on our plan of attack?' he asked her sipping his tea. She looked up at him in bewilderment. 'Now that we've finished upstairs,' he prompted 'we could do the landing, stairs and hallway or we could do the lounge. What's next?'

Sophie allowed herself a moment to stare at him whilst she pretended to think. He really was gorgeous she thought. Why were all the lovely ones unavailable? Life simply wasn't fair.

'I think you were right, lounge next so the rooms are all done. We can finish with the tricky bits.'

'Righto,' he smirked cheerfully. 'You know you don't have to help don't you? Especially with the stairs, they're well, they're awkward.'

'Is this your way of telling me I'm getting in the way?' she smirked at him and began to pick the dried paint from her fingernails.

'Good God no, it's great that you're so...' Andy's words died. As she looked up at him their eyes locked. It was as if time had frozen and they had only just met again, before the skeletons had been found, before she had heard he was already attached, and before any of it, when there were still possibilities.

'...I mean it's good that you want to get involved,' he said levelly. 'I think it's...well it's...good,' he gulped. 'So many people don't...they're...they don't do anything,' he took a deep breath.

Sophie put her mug down on the table and reached for his. Her hand brushed his as she picked it up. She lingered just a split second too long. Andy leant over the table. His lips were soft on hers as he pulled her towards him, his hands cupping her face. The mug handles drifted from her grasp lightly as Andy moved from his seat, pulling her up to her feet. His hands slid down her back slowly and curved her bottom, pulling her towards him even closer. Helplessly she held onto him and their kiss became more intent, the passion erupting like a blaze.

Her fingers created tiny circles on the back of his neck as she kissed him back impatiently. His lips felt like honey. She felt her body melt at his touch. Andy released her and moved his lips onto her neck. Instantly she arched in response to his fluid movements, fitting into his body like a glove. Her soft throaty gasps tumbled into his shoulder like a waterfall as his mouth caressed her neck and his hands stroked her body.

Sophie's eyes flickered open briefly. Her heart leapt into her mouth. She snapped her eyes open and drew back into the table with a light scream. There was a face at the kitchen window. A white hooded face.

'What's wrong?' as he too turned towards the ghostly image pressed up against the glass. The condensation from the intruders breathing fogged up the glass quickly. Sophie breathed heavily and went towards the back door.

'Hello,' she managed to say, straightening her paint-smeared blouse.

'I'm sorry,' the police forensics officer said. 'We tried the bell but there wasn't any answer.'

'Yes, um, I see,' she stammered. 'It's all yours,' she indicated the garden.

'Thank you Miss Harris' the police voice said with a nod. 'I'm sorry to have err, err, disturbed you,' he finished. 'This should be our last day we hope.' She nodded at him quietly. The forensics team were back then she surmised closing the door and turning back into the kitchen. Andy was washing the mugs at the sink and growling silently at the white-coated people that were now sprawling all over the garden like a disease.

'I'm sorry,' she whispered. 'Here, let me,' she offered. 'You don't have to do that.'

'I'm only washing a cup,' he smiled at her. 'It's nothing, really.' She smiled in reply. 'I'd better be going soon,' he said. Reality crashed down on her like a ton of bricks as she nodded, her hair bouncing freely.

'I'm sorry about the paint,' she said, indicating his shirt, the paint from her blouse having merged with his like the butterflies she taught the children to do with folded pages in the classroom.

'That's ok,' he smiled, 'I'm used to being covered in paint, honestly.' There was a silence as he dried his hands on the tea towel. She cowered behind the table, unsure what to say. What did one say to a man one had just kissed passionately who also happened to belong to another women?

'I best get my stuff together,' he said, coming towards her. 'Got to load the van up,' he said, his lips dangerously close to hers again. His fingers brushed her body softly as he passed by towards the staircase. 'Thanks for the tea,' he called as he sprung up the stairs two at a time.

Sophie and Linda selected their favourite of the odd selection for chairs and sat obediently. Linda lowered herself with some difficulty into the largest chair she could find. Usually Glenis, the fat PE teacher, claimed it but since Linda has got so big without the help of chocolate digestives Glenis had had to sacrifice her beloved seat.

'I've got you a little gift,' Sophie said as the others noisily sat down, bags, folders, pens and papers littering the floor like a tidal wave.

'Oh really! I love presents!' Linda giggled. 'What is it?'

'I'm not telling you! You'll have to wait until your maternity leave starts,' Sophie told her with mock sternness.

'Spoil sport,' Linda teased. 'You're looking radiant Soph, what've you done?' Sophie wavered her off with a laugh. 'No, seriously, you look good. Whoever he is, keep him,' Linda smirked.

'Can I have your attention for five minutes please,' the forest tank top and checked shirt were back.

'I'd have thought the tweed police would have caught up with him by now,' Linda scoffed and Sophie tried hard to conceal giggles as the headmaster began his customary rocking on his heels. The room was far too small to hide in and Sophie prayed Linda would keep her whispered jibes quiet for the time being. She felt giddy today and something told her she would have grave difficulty in controlling any happy emotion that came her way.

'I just wanted to check the progress on the fete. Pat, I think you've got the choir started haven't you? What are they singing?'

'Well I'm trying them out on two and we'll sing the one they pick up quickest. Second rehearsal is tonight so I'll let you know tomorrow,' said Pat, his voice booming over the hushed gaggle of teachers.

'Good, good,' the headmaster continued to rock before landing heavily on his toes. Sophie thought he was going to fall forwards but gracefully he applied his mind to the ground just in time. 'Sophie my dear, how is the play going?'

'Well, as Pat said it's second rehearsal tonight. It's a simple story about what Easter eggs mean. I adapted it from the syllabus,' she told him as clearly as possible over the din outside the room where the children were erupting into the playground. 'It's only about ten minutes but we've got five speakers' she concluded. 'I thought we could use the artwork the children did on their return from their Easter break to brighten up the edge of the stage and as markers for the chocolate hunt, Sir.'

'Sounds ideal Sophie my dear, thank you. Marvellous plan. Glenis, could you please oversee the chocolate hunt?' Glenis nodded enthusiastically. 'I may just pop along later to the rehearsal to see how things are going. Well done on the stage by the way,' he addressed Sophie again then surveyed the room with a sweep. 'Have you all seen the magnificent stage Sophie has got for us in the hall?' A murmur wafted around the room. 'Yes, yes, well, good job everyone. Now one last thing,' he rocked dangerously backwards. 'Parents evening is not far away so we've got to make an excellent impression at this fete. I'm sure you'll all do a fantastic job as usual. We want to make all the parents feel welcome, it's vital that they start to take their children's school careers seriously even at this elementary stage. It'll prepare the children and parents alike for secondary school. Right, that's all. Thank you, thank you,' he mumbled, wondering towards the coffee machine and looking gratefully at Glenis to pour a cup for him.

'How's your blood pressure?' Sophie asked Linda as they gathered their bags together and Linda prepared to get up. Sophie took her hands and began to pull her to her feet.

'Ok, thanks honey,' Linda breathed heavily. 'I swear that one day I'll be wedged into that chair and you'll have to cut me free,' she chuckled.

'Oh, Glenis won't like that.' Sophie smirked.

'It's a bit lower apparently,' Linda continued. 'Next scan is next week so fingers crossed it'll still be all right by then.' They made their way to the door, filtering out like sheep into the pen. 'So, how are things with you? The police sorted out those bones yet?' Sophie rolled her eyes with a sigh. 'I take it that's a no then. Don't worry honey, they can't be much longer now. It'll all come right, you'll see.' Sophie smiled at Linda, she was a fabulous friend, unlimited faith and right now, she thought, she could do with hitching a ride on Linda's faith because her own had dwindled. Andy kissing her had livened it up considerably but that was just a moment, she reminded herself. The blush was filling her face and she felt hotter. Linda eyed her suspiciously. 'Something you want to tell me Miss?' her eyebrows arched mockingly. Sophie shook her head, abashed at being caught out.

'No, no, I'm fine,' she lied, held her head up and opened the door of the staff room. 'Besides the police were there yesterday afternoon and they said they're 99% done so the whole nightmare should be over soon. Apparently,' she continued, shuffling out the door way and holding it wide for Linda to pass her, 'they've got everything they can get from the "site" as they call it. So there's not much more they can do now but wait for the test results. Listen, I'd better get going,' the bell sounded loudly, 'that's double English coming up. Catch ya later,' she flashed a smile at Linda that was brighter than she felt. 'I'm fine, honest,' she said hugging Linda quickly.

'Um right, whatever you say then,' Linda laughed. 'See you later.'

Sophie's day was and felt long and dull. The bell finally tolled but not for her. It was time for the second rehearsal.

The sunlight hid momentarily behind a cloud, bathing the school hall in a large grey shadow. Sophie eyed her own silhouette on the floor as she entered the hall, the only stream of sunlight flooded in through the far window, dancing just at her feet spontaneously. She flicked the light switches and the shadow dance died.

'Hello Miss, hello Miss,' a chorus of squawks echoed loudly as the children ran into the hall towards the stage, climbing up with more energy than they ever demonstrated in their PE classes, according to Glenis anyway. Sophie flashed them her professional smile and walked briskly towards the gathering crowd on the stage.

'Now, children, we've got to practice the play again. You did really well last week so we'll just go over it again to make sure you can remember it and then we'll start working on the background scenery.' Her collection of clipboards with photocopied lines pinned to them clattered to the floor of the stage. The children grabbed theirs possessively and took their places on the stage. 'Let's see what we can find to help you get into character shall we.' Sophie opened the bulging dressing-up cupboard at the side of the hall. Lost somewhere into the depths of the costume rack she managed to unearth some hats and capes. Not really suitable but they may just create a difference between reading lines and acting.

The children rushed to select their favourites and assembled on the stage like a wild mismatched group. Sophie suppressed a light giggle. They were so sweet at that young age. Pity they had to grow up really. Never the same once they hit secondary school.

'Right, good, let's start from the top. So, first the...' She gestured wildly hoping against the odds that they would remember or read their lines without her prompting.

'Uuurgh! Uuurgh!'

'Yes, well done that's it. Now carry on,' she smiled, relieved at their enthusiasm, and settled down to her task of background scenery. A patchwork quilt effect, only this one would be made of coloured card and sequins, painted pictures from their own art lessons and held together with string and staples. It had to stretch across the entire back wall and was meant to represent the Easter egg wrapping.

'Go on then,' the children continued 'tell us, what do Easter eggs mean then?'

'They mean chocolate!' Jimmy shouted, his arms waving madly about his head. 'Lots of lovely chocolate!'

'Yeah, shaped like eggs,' Lucy cried. Sophie watched the children impressed with their sheer exhilaration for the play. She hadn't realised they would take it so seriously. Still, no complaints she thought, made her job easier.

'I bet you don't know where they come from though do you?' Annabel was pouting and put her hands on her hips with a cheeky grin.

'The chocolate factory?' Peter volunteered.

'No, no, no,' Annabel insisted, again resting her hands on her hips defiantly. She really was very good. Andy was right; she was a natural actress Sophie mused, fiddling with her cardboard stitching uselessly. 'Not chocolate eggs, the real eggs!'

Sophie noticed the headmaster creeping in at the back of the hall. The children hadn't seen him. She nodded at him subtly and continued with her stitching.

'Oh real eggs, they come from chickens,' piped up little Lisa, her voice quiet.

'Yeah, why did the donkey cross the road?' Jimmy suddenly asked.

'You mean why did the chicken cross the road?' Lucy argued

'No, it was the chicken's day off!' Jimmy quipped and they all laughed. Sophie sat watching, quietly impressed with her little play. It was going much better than she had expected. The headmaster beamed brightly; always a good sign.

'Are you going to tell us then?' Lisa turned towards Annabel.

'If you stop being silly,' Annabel held her chin high in indignation.

'Sorry,' came the chorus from Jimmy, Peter and Lucy.

'Tell us, please,' said Lisa.

'Ok,' Annabel began as they all sat down. 'If you left the egg with the chicken what would happen?'

'Little chicks,' Lisa said, 'sweet little chicks would come out of them.'

'That's right,' Annabel waved her finger at them all convincingly and picked up her clipboard to find her next line. 'Yes, life would be the result. New life. So that's what Easter is all about.'

'I don't get it,' Jimmy said, dropping his clipboard loudly on the floor of the wooden stage. Sophie nearly jumped.

'New life,' Annabel said again. 'Easter is the time we remember that Jesus came back to life so we can have a new life.'

'Wow, I never knew that,' Lucy said.

'So the egg gives us new life, I get it,' Peter said.

'Eggs-exactly,' Jimmy quipped and they all laughed.

Sophie stood up and clapped her hands. The headmaster joined her and clapped loudly. Jimmy took a bow and the headmaster laughed. A deep boisterous laugh. It seemed strange that the tweed character should have a sense of humour at all. Sophie twisted her face towards the children quickly so as not to stare.

'That was perfect children, just perfect. Now, do you think you can do it without your clipboards next week? Can you try to remember your lines?'

'Yes Miss, yes Miss, yes Miss.'

'Wonderful. Ok, well you can go home I think. Your mums and dads should be waiting just out in the corridor, I'll go check,' she ventured towards the doors as the headmaster knelt down to talk to his star performers.

Sophie opened the hall doors and scanned the corridor. A gaggle of parents were huddled in from the rain, gossiping and mingling. She swung open the doors to the full capacity and hooked the catches in place.

'Ok, ok,' she called as loudly as she could but the parents were too busy chatting. 'You can go in now,' she said quietly to the nearest couple to her and watched them lead the way, the rest following in a rush to get their child and go home. As the parents filed into the hall she stood by the door, the usual pleasantries.

'Yes, thank you Mrs Furkins...yes, Peter is doing wonderfully well...um yes...thank you...hello Mr Mantra...yes of course, thank you...'

'Hello,'

Sophie's heart leapt up into her mouth.

'How is she doing?' he asked, coming round from behind her towards the door.

'Daddy!' Annabel ran towards them and Andy lowered to catch her in his arms. 'Daddy! I did it didn't I Miss Harris?'

'You did very well' Sophie heard herself say. 'Very good, you'll be great,' she smiled at Annabel and tried desperately not to look at her father.

'Can we go home now Daddy, mummy said she'd get ice-cream today, can we please?' Andy picked his daughter up so she was looking over his shoulder towards the main entrance to the school. He flashed a smile at Sophie and she felt the flush fill her face again instantly.

'Come on then you,' he looked at Annabel, 'have you got your bags?'

'Yes Daddy, yes Daddy, hurry up because mummy said I could have ice-cream today...'

Sophie watched them leave numbly until there was nothing left to watch, only the clouds darkening, burdened with rain.

The bath crystals crackled and disintegrated as they fell into the hot bubbly water. Sophie added another sprinkle liberally and watched lavender wisps float around the steady stream as she poured the bubble bath mixture under the running hot water. It was only eight o'clock but it had been a long day and she knew she needed to sleep. After the rehearsal she had come home, her emotions tormenting her all the way, his secret smile, the fact that he was already taken… But that secret smile, it meant something, what did it mean?

She had eaten a tasteless microwave meal through sheer exhaustion and inability to drum up encouragement to cook something real. She had marked the weekly homework papers with the customary red ink slumped into the sofa and watched a repeat of Porridge on BBC2.

Now, as she dipped her toes into the steamy bubbles and settled down she wondered why she hadn't headed straight for the bathroom. The soft lightening from the hallway was all she needed, leaving the bathroom door ajar and laying in the peace and quiet, allowing the coconut soap bar to glide over her pink wet skin effortlessly.

Sophie knew two things for sure. One, the police were now finished with her garden but the results were not going to be pleasant. She had to face facts; somewhere in her family history lay tragedy and it was about to surface. Two, she was already far too deeply in love with Andy Taylor that trouble was just around the corner. She was diving head first into emotional disaster and she couldn't stop herself. She knew with ultimate certainty that if he were here with her right now, she would kiss him again. She knew, despite all logic and reason, that she couldn't resist him any longer. It was against her power now.

Make the most of the peace and quiet she told herself, *because it isn't going to last long!*

15th April 2009   Issue No 1910
ATWOOD CHRONICLE

Buried Victims Named

The exact location of the 'bodies beneath the lawn' remains a secret known only by our diligent local police force. Following the gruesome discovery by a local woman of two skeletons beneath the neatly kept lawn, we're still no closer to being privy to the location of this unusual burial place. Our article regarding this discovery was in one of our March editions, issue number 1821, and told you originally that the time of the burial was dated some years ago. We can now confirm burial took place in 1935, long before our current resident moved into the property. Death occurred only hours before the burial was made, local police scientist report. "Rigour-mortis had not fully set in before the bodies were submerged in the earth. We know this from the speed of decay. Modern technology helps us to determine exactly how long a body remains subject to oxygen before burial occurs. In this case we are fortunate. The bodies were preserved sufficiently before burial occurred, and identity and cause of death can be obtained from the remains."

The relatively new house owner, who remains anonymous for the sake of privacy, has refused to allow her address to become public domain for this story. I don't blame her either, it's bound to attract a crowd!

The skeletons consisted of the remains of two people buried in 1935, namely Elise Harris and Thomas Brody. Both deaths are still being treated as suspicious, although no arrests have been made.

Elise Harris was a former resident of the property where her body was found. Thomas Brody was a local man, whose absence had been highlighted to police shortly after his death. The connection between them is still sketchy to say the least, but police are confident a connection will come to light. "We know there will be a link between the two individuals, there always is!" WPC Clarke, spokeswoman for the local police constabulary told us. "We just have to be patient. This case has a long history even before the skeletons were found, dating back now to the time of death; the motive for which is still unclear."

If you can help with the investigation in any way contact your local police station immediately. We'll keep you up to date with the latest as we receive it.

Chapter Eight

I am sitting by my window again, thinking back on a happier time. May has always been my most favourite month. The expectant summer warmth floats into our lives like a whispered prayer.

The birds are singing and the rain freshens up the grass to leave us dew ready for a new day, a clean day. Everything is clear, the clouds crisp in their outlines and the trees and flowers blossoming before our very eyes. I am thinking about Tom. He bought me a Milky Way, it's brand new and we had to queue for twenty minutes to get one. I smile to myself at this simple memory. It sounds silly but even the most basic things are wonderful with Tom. I love him you see. I feel empty when he's not by my side. My life has no meaning when he goes home and I ache with missing him. I'm not exaggerating. It's true. I think I've always known this. I was nervous, especially at first.

I remember the desperation for each other that launched us into a full-blown affair. It was never my intention to betray my husband – despite his flaws, nor do I believe he ever planned to be unfaithful to his wife. Tom's wife is a toff. She has money, lots of it, inherited easily. She lives out her days in a state of intoxication, champagne running through her veins on a daily basis. Tom told me yesterday that she had just bought an Austin 7, the old car "was out of fashion" apparently. Sometimes I wonder if she even notices that he isn't there. Still, that doesn't excuse our behaviour. We couldn't help it. It just happened and there was little we could do to stop it.

107

Emotion had overpowered us and we had to have each other –
it was that simple.

'It will cross the line,' he warned me. 'As much as I want
you, I need to know you will be able to live with that
afterwards.' At that moment I looked up into his eyes and he
held me tighter than ever before. 'It's more than anything
we've ventured so far,' he said again. 'I'll be all right, but I
need to know you will be too.' I remember kissing him
tenderly and nodding my head at his every word.

'I'll cope,' I told him. 'I'll find a way to cope.'

Three full days of not seeing each other followed and I
ached for him, paced rooms silently and fidgeted, restless for
his touch. It was almost too much for my weak heart to bear.
Finally the day came and he was due to visit the house. This
wasn't normal but I knew Frederick would be away that day
and there was little if any danger of him coming home.
Clarissa always went out on Fridays. I had given the staff an
unexpected day off and warned them – out of earshot from my
husband or mother-in-law not to return before six.

'Did you miss me?' I asked as I moved closer into him.
His shirt was pale blue. I ran my finger along one of the
delicately woven stripes, etching along his chest. I quivered as
he pulled me into him, his arms fixed around me tightly.

'Course, silly question,' I heard him muffle into my hair.
'You smell so good,' he whispered. We stood for a while, his
back against the windowsill. I wondered what would happen
next, would he politely back off like the previous encounters?

'How long have you got?' I asked his shirt.

'I will have to leave about five I guess.'

The silence was heavy but comfortable.

'Why doesn't this feel wrong?' I asked him, nestled as I
was into his chest.

'I don't know,' he answered honestly. We had always been
honest with each other; it was the one quality that kept us
apart, until now.

The warmth of his fingers tracing my jaw-line spread
through me like a blaze. He tilted my head and I looked into

his eyes, my own reflection starring back at me like a mirror. I moved my arms around his neck as he leant into me, his breath warm on my face as his lips parted. He kissed me tenderly, his hands cupping my face and mine circling his back, settling finally in the rear pockets of his dark navy trousers. Then he moved me, my head to one side as he began massaging my neck with his mouth. The tremors skipped through me like shock waves, lighting me up from the inside.

'Hmm…' a soft murmur from him as his lips caressed my throat and slid around to my left side. I held onto him hard, feeling light as if I would melt into a pool on the floor at any moment. 'Take off your stockings for me,' he whispered into my ear. Reluctantly I backed away, our fingers entwined until I neared the light of the open doorway.

My heart leapt wildly as I slipped into the bathroom. I tossed the stockings into the laundry hamper quickly, straightened my hair as smoothly as I could with my palms and took a deep breath. Did I really want to do this? It took seconds to decide that I did. I knew it was wrong but I wanted it badly. This could be the only opportunity to ever present itself. What was I waiting for? I took another deep breath.

When I looked at him in the room, he was starring out the window. He turned at the sound of my bare feet padding across the carpet; his arms outstretched drawing me in like a magnet. I couldn't help myself and he knew it.

Instantly our passion began, his tongue exploring my mouth with vigour, his hands all over me, searching, finding, caressing.

'Sit over there' his voice was breathless. I sat on the edge of the bed and he knelt before me, his face level with mine, his hands swiftly freeing me of my chiffon blouse, over my head it went barely without my noticing. He kissed me again as his fingers effortlessly unclipped my corset. 'Hmm…' another barely audible gasp as my undergarments fell between us. His lips closed on my left breast, his right hand removing the white lacy garment and tossing it to one side. 'You're beautiful,' he whispered, his hands caressing my body, his fingers light to the touch, his hot lips tender as they covered me quickly.

I felt my heart skip a beat, my breath caught in my throat. My resolve was well and truly melted. There was nothing I could do but play to his mercy. I looked into his eyes, their brightness glistening, reaching into my very soul, penetrating my fears and puncturing them easily. I had played this story over in my mind a thousand times and each time I had been shy, hesitant, but surprisingly I wasn't either of those things. Nobody had ever made me feel like this before.

'Are you sure?' he asked, drawing me back towards him. Incapable of speech I nodded silently, fiddling with the buttons on his shirt as he removed his jacket. 'I should stop but I can't,' he confessed, his naked chest revealed to me for the first time. I ran my hands over it; the smooth texture was warm to my touch, his nipples hardened at my fingertips.

Firmly and with control he pushed me backwards, shuffled me into a position where he could raise my skirt, my white underwear inches from his mouth. I watched in fascination as he stroked my thighs, my knickers, and then smoothly proceeded to remove them completely. His lips moved closer to me, his tongue caressing me gently. Deep sighs escaped me as I clawed at the edge of the bed in an effort to keep still. Such delicate tender touch, and yet a tornado sped through me relentlessly, mercilessly, and I bit my tongue as it hurtled to a halt. The passion I felt for him was so urgent, so desperate... helpless.

In the dusk-lit room I watched the awakening moon shine across his head, his face half bathed in the moonlight. His hands were everywhere, his finger probing further and further into my depths. Before I realised it he had drawn me close again, moved me to the floor and pulled me on top of him. I kissed him hard, resting my hand beneath his head.

'I don't know what you like,' he whispered, his eyes shone by the moonlight.

'So find out,' I whispered, reaching for him and rolling him over to one side. He began kissing my legs, raising my feet in the air and knelt up, parted my legs and then he was there. I drew him closer to me, wrapping my legs around his body. Each movement he made sent vibrations through me.

110

My fingers encircled his chest as he moved quickly, then slowly; then he paused.

'My God, you're perfect,' his hoarse whispering lips dancing close to mine.

I kissed him in response and his speed increasing rapidly. 'This is all for you,' his voice was raspy as he thrust against me, the rocketing sensation clasping around us as he rested on top of me. I kissed him gently. 'Well I think we've crossed the line now,' he whispered and I smiled.

Slowly he got up. 'May I use your bathroom?'

'Of course,' my voice was quiet. I stumbled to my feet and clutched at a fresh black dress from the wardrobe.

'Why are you hiding?' he peered around the wardrobe door.

'I don't know,' I answered as he fetched his clothes. 'Your shirt,' I said, untangling it from my undergarments with slight difficulty. He took it with a smile and headed for the bathroom. In the moments that followed I am not sure what I did, but I know I did something; something to distract me from the thoughts buzzing around my mind.

I heard him leave the bathroom. Quickly I washed and swiftly dressed, throwing on the black dress and tossing the skirt and blouse into the laundry hamper. I would have to deal with my thoughts later. It was too late to go back now but I knew immediately that had I to re-live the day I wouldn't have changed it at all.

He sat on the long seat in the sitting room, the brightness in stark contrast to the previous dusky moments. His bow tie was draped around his neck and he held his half-drunk tea cup. I sat next to him, stroked his trouser encased leg and looked at him. He smiled at me. I leant into him, resting against him.

'Well that will never happen again,' he said, half looking down at me, 'or maybe…' his sentence hung in the air between us. I let it be.

'Are you ok?' I asked, not looking at his face.

'Yes, may not be in half an hour!' His smile was radiant. 'You?'

'I think so.'

'I kept my socks on,' he confessed. 'Terrible habit.'

'I didn't notice,' I half laughed.

'No, didn't think so.' He stroked my arm repeatedly. 'I'll have to go in a minute,' he said, avoiding my eyes. I nodded again, watching him stroking my arm.

Reluctantly we stood up. He put the empty tea cup on the silver tray and returned for his coat and shoes. I joined him in the hallway.

'I will ring you over the weekend,' he said, 'I'll find a couple of minutes.' I understood.

'Ok.' Closing in for a last cuddle I felt him hold me tighter than ever. 'I'll see you next week,' my voice beginning to crack.

'It's going to be a long four days,' he said. With that I opened the door and he was gone.

Chapter Nine

April 2009

The alarm clock ticked over slowly, counting down the minutes until it's shrill tone punctured Sophie's sleep like a knife. She lay twisted up in the sheets, her dreams delighting her beyond her wildest expectations.

Ring, ring, ring

No, no, she thought, the phone isn't ringing; it wouldn't ever disturb us at such a point in dreamland...

Ring, ring, ring... she sprang up like a cat. It was her phone. Wearily she rubbed her eyes and looked at the clock. Half past five!

'Hello,' she whispered hoarsely into the receiver.

'Sophie baby, it's me, listen babes, I'm in a spot of bother; you know me.' A crisp half laugh crackled down the line. 'I need you to come down to the station and bail me out, can you do that for me baby, for old time's sake?'

Sophie took the receiver away from her ear and stared at it incredulously. The voice at the other end was still going.

'Baby, you still there? You see you're the only one who can save me. Please baby, please...are you there?'

'Yes I'm here but I'm not your baby anymore so no, I can't bail you out. Why don't you get one of your current victims to rescue you, you selfish spoilt brat!' she spat into the phone and replaced the receiver with a thump that made her jump. She dove under the covers furiously tossing and turning until, knotted into anger, she gave in and got up. She padded angrily down to the kitchen and flicked on the kettle. It was still only six o'clock in the morning, indecently early for her to

113

ring Linda. How dare he! How bloody dare he ring and ask her for money! She threw the teabag into her favourite mug and poured the hot water over quickly. The sheer cheek of it! The milk plopped into the mug in splashes and she threw the container back into the fridge door and slammed the fridge shut.

Then she took a sip of tea, nearly burnt her mouth as she gulped it down at speed and ventured into the lounge where she plonked herself onto the sofa and curled up into a ball.

Joe was history and he was certainly going to stay that way. She didn't want, nor need, him cluttering up her life. She was perfectly capable of making a mess of it by herself - without his help.

Why didn't he ask the gorgeous Lynette anyway, or perhaps she too had been relegated to the ranks of history in his never-ending stream of one-night affairs? He wasn't above building a harem for himself; at least he didn't used to be. She felt sure there were at least six current flames of his, equally oblivious to the real Joe, whom he could turn to.

Sophie drank her tea silently seething and willing her mind to go blank. He wasn't worth it she reminded herself. He simply wasn't worth her anger, her time, and certainly not her money. Let him bail himself out for a change. She took the last sip of tea and a deep breath. It was almost time to get up now so she headed for the bathroom and vowed not to think about him anymore.

'Good morning,' she heard him say, that sultry sexy voice over her shoulder. She turned sharply to find him smiling at her, Annabel holding his hand.

The chatter surrounded them. Children's excited shrills and screams and parents hushed commands. Younger brothers and sisters in prams and pushchairs, mums rocking them to sleep whilst calling after the older child to stop running or pulling at the little girl's skirt.

'Morning,' she said, 'good morning Annabel,' she smiled down at the little girl briefly. 'I' have to...'

'Sure, see you later,' his eyes sparkled at her. Sophie turned towards the school doors but not before she saw Annabel's mother approaching them. Quickly she forced her mind into gear and almost ran across the playground towards the staff room. She didn't want to see Annabel's mother. She didn't want to see them together. What was happening to her?

'Hi,' Linda chirped 'how's you?'

'I'm fine,' Sophie answered, dropping her bags into a heap, glad beyond relief to be somewhere normal.

'Oh, that good huh. No, you're not, spill,' Linda commanded. 'I'll get the coffee.' Sophie sighed heavily. How on earth did Linda always know?

'It's nothing. Really.'

'No it's not, it's never nothing when you say that. You're like a jack in a box lately. Come on, out with it,' Linda placed two mugs of steaming coffee at the table and Sophie sat at Linda's command.

'Joe rang this morning,' she said quietly.

'Oh my God, what'd he want?' Linda gasped.

'He wanted me to "bail him out, for old times sake", at half past five this morning,' she flicked her fingers into speech marks. Linda sipped her coffee, for once stunned into silence. 'Isn't he still with Lynette?'

Linda looked at her levelly.

'I don't know honey, I haven't been talking to her much since it er, happened. No sister of mine behaves so badly without reason and far as I can tell she doesn't have a reason.'

'Hey, I'm sorry,' Sophie put her hand on Linda's arm and Linda patted it. 'I never wanted you to lose your sister over it, I swear!'

'I know honey,' Linda soothed. 'We weren't that close anyway. Never really understood her. She's probably not seeing him anymore. Mum said she was screwing around with this other guy so maybe they've broken up. Anyway, I don't care about her, well, I do really, you know what I mean. I care about you. You didn't though, did you?'

'Didn't what? Bail him out? What are you, mad? This pregnancy has affected your mind if you think I'd fall for that after all the crap he put me through!' Sophie scoffed and the women giggled.

'Good, see, I was right,' Linda nodded her head proudly. 'Told you it'd be fine. He's history and you know it.'

'Yeah, though perhaps I'll change my phone number,' Sophie smiled at her. 'We'd better get moving. The kids are being let in,' Sophie nodded towards the window as the crowd outside began flooding in vociferously through the doors. Yelps were heard in the corridor. Another day begins Sophie thought. Here we go again. It can only get better.

The sunlight was strong, dicing the hall into sections under its rays. Pat stood on his heels surveying the choir before him as if they were the royal harmonic. The children were singing loudly but all in varying keys. Their little mouths were projecting the hymns out over the empty hall with great enthusiasm. Relegated to the far corner of the stage was Sophie's merry band of actors; going through their lines blissfully unaware of the forthcoming din that was bound to ensue.

'Are you ready Miss Harris?' Pat's voice bounced over the practising choir's heads and Sophie nodded in reply. Let battle commence.

'Right ok my little cherubs,' Pat bought his arms up to silence the choir. 'We're going to practice that again but this time our players will be acting out in front. So' he gestured towards the back of the stage. 'Take a step backwards everyone to make room for the players. Miss Harris, we're ready for you.'

Sophie led her little team to the centre stage and they assembled into place in front of the choir.

'Right ok,' Pat said again. 'Miss Harris take it away. Right children, we're going to sing the first one again but this time very quietly so the players can be heard over us. Ready, on three. One, two three…' The choir began to sing, loudly, as Pat lowered his arms frantically like a bird trying to fly with broken wings. 'Sssh…quietly' he whispered bringing his fingers to his lips. 'Sssh…'

116

'Good, that's right Annabel,' Sophie said quietly. 'From the start.'

As the play came into perfection Sophie sat back with her patchwork scenery and watched as Pat, still conducting his choir, gestured for them to get louder as the play came to a close and they started on the last hymn, clearly allowing for every conceivable key to be heard by the unsuspecting audience.

It was almost seven when the doorbell chimed and Sophie let Andy in. He wore a pair of paint-splattered jeans and a white t-shirt that clung to his body like a second skin. Even in the fading sun of the cool spring temperature Sophie suddenly felt hot in his presence.

'Hi,' she breathed as she swung the door wide open, her eyes cast over his torso as he entered her home, his fingers clutching pots of paint, rollers and dust sheets.

'Hiya, I thought we could do with a bit more,' he said indicating the tins in his grasp. 'We're almost there but I hate to be running low on paint,' he explained as he strolled into the lounge. 'This room will take a bit longer than the bedrooms but we've got a good couple of hours tonight and we'll be a good way through it by the weekend I should think,' he was saying as he unloaded the tins and the dust sheets. 'Do you mind if we move the furniture to the middle of the room?'

'No, no, of course not,' she agreed. 'Sorry I should have...'

'Don't be daft woman, here, let me take that,' he took a strong hold of the end of the settee and dragged it into the centre of the carpet. 'So, how was the rehearsal today?' he asked her, his voice muffled by the end of the sofa.

'Good, good. Annabel is really coming along, I expect you're proud of her,' she said, her voice softening at the sparkle in his eyes. 'She's a natural.'

'Do you really think so? I can't imagine where she gets it from, certainly not from me, must be her mother,' he smiled. Sophie hid her face quickly behind a cushion.

'Yes, perhaps,' she whispered. She didn't want to think about Annabel's mother. 'Are you still going to be able to make it to the fete?' she asked, springing up from behind the bookcase.

'I'll take that, it's too heavy for you,' he commanded, 'you can take those lamps there. Yes, I'll be there,' he smiled. 'She'd never forgive me if I missed it!' he laughed heartily and Sophie found herself smiling.

The furniture now sat heaped in the centre of the room and Andy began to unfold the dust sheets. He flung one over the furniture pile and tossed a few casually around the exposed carpet.

The telephone rang. Sophie looked at it and glanced at Andy with a shy smile.

'Hello,' she breathed into the receiver still watching Andy through the open lounge doorway moving smoothly about the lounge.

'Can I speak to Miss Harris please?'

'Speaking'

'It's Sergeant Wells here Miss Harris, from Ipswich station, Suffolk Constabulary. I've been asked to give you an update on the remains recovered from your garden.'

'Yes?'

'We now believe the cause of death to be stabbing. There are grazes on the rib cage bones consistent with a short sharp blade. It's highly probable that the blade punctured the heart. It could easily be the same knife for both skeletons, but of course it's too late to be sure.'

'Right,' Sophie said, unsure how to react. 'Thank you for letting me know.'

'Excuse me Miss but I'm also instructed to ask if our inspector could pop along to see you tomorrow. He has one or two further questions, nothing to worry about.'

'Yes of course,' she said. 'I'll be home from work by 5, is there any chance of his coming after that?'

'I'll make that clear Miss, yes, thank you for your time. Goodnight Miss Harris.'

'Goodnight Sergeant.'

Andy was covering large areas of the living room walls in a sugar soap mixture, the bubbling spray raining over the dust sheets liberally. It smelt sweet like candy-floss. Sophie inhaled deeply and picked up a dry brush, rubbed the bristles across her palm and cast Andy a smile brighter than she felt.

'That was the police,' she told him idly hopping from one foot to the other. 'The inspector wants to ask me more questions tomorrow. Apparently the skeletons were stabbed to death,' she announced. Andy watched her cautiously. 'Listen, do you think we could do the garden after the decorating is finished, after all?' she asked, still playing with the dry brush. Andy nodded as he stretched up high with the soap laden brush in hand. 'I was thinking that now the garden is free to touch again, I'd like it to look different. It's like an earthquake at the moment since the police dug it up. Apparently they had to take soil samples to test how long the bones had been in the ground or something like that. Anyway, every time I look out there I remember.'

'Sure, we won't be too long doing this. Tell you what, I'll get Bill onto it whilst I'm away.'

'Away?' she panicked, dropping the dry brush on the floor with a dull thud. 'What do you mean away?'

'I was going to tell you tonight anyway' he said, 'that client I told you about, the one I was trying to win…'

'Oh yes, I've got your reference,' she scuttled off into the kitchen and returned with a cream envelope, neatly written on the front in blue fountain pen was Andy's name. 'Here' she said, 'I'll leave it with your keys by the door.'

'Thanks,' he said 'I've got to go and meet with them at their head office. I'll only be gone a few days so I promise we won't get behind with the work here,' he smiled taking a step towards her. 'Bill can start on the garden and we'll pick up the rest of the painting when I get back,' he said, drawing even closer to her gradually.

'Oh I know that, I wasn't thinking about the work… I meant I don't want you to go away' she covered her mouth quickly. 'I mean…I mean it won't be the same without…I mean…' Sophie stammered then gave up. The scarlet shade flushed her face instantly as she spun around, her eyes scanning the dishevelled room desperately for somewhere to hide.

'Thank you,' his voice was quiet and tranquil as he put the brush down and came towards her. 'Really means a lot to me.' His arms slid around her waist as she fit into his lean body easily. Sophie breathed in quickly but found her arms on his shoulders, was it possible for her own body to betray her better judgement... she looked into his eyes and knew at that moment she was not capable of resisting him, however inappropriate, however wrong she knew it to be. Andy's eyes smiled at her. He lifted her chin with his finger and cupped her face with the warmth of his palm. His body warmth penetrated her until she felt light, all will power melted into oblivion. Slowly his lips came closer to hers until she felt his breath tickling her face, teasing her with expectation. She kissed him first; the familiar excitement of him made her feel giddy. The sheer exhilaration of his touch made her pulse race, her eyes glaze and her mind settle into bliss as he kissed her back passionately, his hands roaming the small of her back, his fingers circling her body recklessly.

Andy squeezed her tighter to him and entwined her hair in his fingers.

'I guess we'd better get this painting finished,' he sighed reluctantly. 'This isn't very professional of me is it,' he whispered. She half smiled at him as he kissed her on the forehead and resumed the sugar-soaping. Sophie put the radio on and Tina Turner *what's love got to do with it* sang at them loudly. They worked quickly, each aware of what they could be doing when the painting were concluded...

'When do you leave?' she asked, her eyes fixed on the paint she was applying to the far wall, her back to him.

'Tomorrow,' he said shortly.

'Oh.'

'I'll send Bill in. He's a nice guy. I'll ask him to tidy up the garden. That'll keep him busy for a couple of days. I'm only away two nights,' he assured her.

'Just two,' she repeated, 'good luck,' she offered 'with the new client I mean.'

'Thanks.'

'I may change my phone number whilst you're away,' she told him, 'but I'll text you the new one if I do.'

'Oh?'

'It's nothing really, but a part of history has the number and I'd rather he didn't.'

'Sorry.'

'Don't be. It wasn't a problem until the other day when he rang at five thirty in the morning asking me to bail him out of jail. I sure know how to pick them!' she half laughed. 'Anyway, I'll text you if it changes whilst you're away.'

Andy looked around at her incredulous.

'Bail him out?' he questioned. 'You're serious?'

'Afraid so,' she said, not trusting herself to return his glance and furiously painting. Andy continued painting.

'Do you want to talk about it?' he said into the wall that was now turning into a peaceful shade of honey.

'There's not much to tell,' she said, her voice quieter and her hand working slower. 'We dated in university, he had a string of affairs that I was too blind to notice, too naïve to believe.'

'What happened?' Andy asked, now giving up on the paint and facing her.

'He started seeing this one girl, behind my back, she knew of course that he was supposed to be with me. She was my best friend's sister.' Andy's eyebrow shot up in support. 'Anyway, they were seeing each other. I managed to stumble across them when they were...' Sophie's voice died.

'Sorry Soph,' he said, taking her hand in his.

'Yeah, well,' she shrugged. 'We broke up, I finished university, he dropped out before final exams I think, and I haven't seen or heard from him since, until the other morning.'

'You deserve much better than that,' he smiled at her, took up his brush and continued to paint the far wall. 'It's a good idea, to change your number, I'd do it if I were you.' The best of the eighties one hit wonders were playing on the radio as the DJ counted down to number one.

Sophie painted on, wondering what Andy thought about men like Joe. After all, hadn't he just kissed her, was he really any better? Linda had told her not to mention Joe but that was before, when she didn't know who Andy was. When Andy was a possibility, not a far-fetched fantasy that would probably lead to disaster. Anyway, she reasoned to herself, Andy and her, so they'd kissed a couple of times. It wasn't as if they'd torn their clothes off...how she wanted to...no, she commanded herself, no, she wouldn't allow it to go any further. He was unavailable. If it had been Joe he'd have gone five steps beyond the finale in the first ten minutes. No, they weren't alike at all. She chastised herself for even comparing the two. Andy was a gentleman who happened to find her attractive. He couldn't help it any more than she could.

'How are you getting on over there?' he cut into her thoughts with a bright smile. 'We're almost done with the first coat I think,' he beamed. 'I could whiz round in the morning and do the second coat if you like, that way it'll be done before I have to go.'

'That would be brilliant but I'll be at work tomorrow,' she sighed

'You could er, leave me a key?' he suggested

'Oh yes, absolutely. Good idea,' she rushed out to fetch her keys. 'Are you sure you don't mind? I don't want to make you late for your big meeting,' she said fiddling with the keys on the key-chain.

'Here, let me,' he took the keys from her, his fingers brushing over hers lightly. With ease he removed the key she indicated and handed the chain back to her. 'Thanks,' he said. 'Do you want me to put the furniture back for the time being or can it wait until tomorrow?'

'Tomorrow,' she purred

Andy held her close, smelt her hair and stroked her back.

'Life just isn't fair is it,' she whispered.

'Ssh...' he kissed the top of her head. 'I'll be back real soon, I promise.'

Sophie paced her scruffy garden anxiously. The police inspector was due any minute to interrogate her some more. It wasn't as if she even knew anything of any use. Previously she had been scared they would link the murders to her family but after all this time all she really wanted was for it all to be over, for the mystery to be solved so she could dig over the garden and forget about the whole ghastly affair.

The inspector was a tall man with a nose that looked suspiciously as if it had been in a fight, and lost. It had healed badly. Sophie tried not to stare. Inspector Allen wore a stained Macintosh the colour of burnt toast. It hung limply open revealing a grey worn suit and a thread-bare blue scarf, despite the spring sunshine.

'Good evening Miss Harris,' he began in a deep voice. He puffed incessantly on a cigarette as he approached her from the side gate. 'I'm sorry to trouble you, just one or two things I need to clear up for my report.' The inspector spun round. 'Where's that lad? Sergeant, where are you son?'

Sergeant Wells, a short stout man of senior years trotted around the side of the house, notebook and pencil already in hand. He came to the inspector's side, still catching his breath.

'Yes sir?'

'Now, take this down man. Miss Harris,' the inspector addressed her again. A strange urge to stand to attention washed over Sophie. Instead she cast him a sly smile and glanced back down at the mess the uniformed police constables had made of the garden. 'Can you tell me anymore about the previous occupiers of the house Miss, we're particularly looking at your great grandfather's brother, a...' the inspector looked towards his Sergeant quizzically.

'Frederick, Sir.'

'Thank you, Wells. A Frederick Harris, brother Rodney Harris I believe.'

'I'm sorry Inspector but I really don't know how I can help you. I knew my grandmother of course, but beyond that I simply don't know. I wasn't around...'

'Yes yes, of course. How about your parents Miss Harris, might they know?'

123

'I've asked them. You see Frederick would have been my father's great uncle but Frederick and Rodney didn't get along very well so…'

'I see. Well, we'll have to do it the hard way then. It was worth a shot anyway.'

'What was? Do you know who they were? The last note I received referred to Elise.' Sophie eyed the inspector carefully in case he was holding back but he didn't even finch.

'Yes, we wondered about that. Elise was Frederick's wife wasn't she?'

'Yes inspector.'

'It could be Elise of course, there is no death certificate for her and she must have died after all these years. That's certainly the trail we're following. Frederick is buried in the graveyard at the top of the town, we've checked and his death is recorded in all the appropriate places. His wife, however, is not mentioned at all. We're quite confident that the female remains belong to Elise but the male remains don't appear to belong to your family tree.'

'The other family members all have death certificates I suppose?' she asked, shivering slightly. The sun was setting slowly and a shadow cast the inspectors face in a strange half light. He blew a perfect smoke ring, admired it keenly and looked back at Sophie.

'Yes Miss, we've checked and double-checked. The male remains can't possibly be any of your family, so who else was around at the time…' The inspector looked towards Sergeant Wells and puffed on his diminishing cigarette.

'No, nothing Sir, we've got no known associates for Elise.'

'The newspaper mentioned a name…' Sophie began.

'Yes, yes, no idea how they got that,' Inspector Allen said.

'We're checking. Any other thoughts Miss Harris?'

'No, I'm sorry inspector. My parents have no idea I'm afraid. I did ask but as I said…'

'Yes, yes. Ok, we'll have to trawl through the missing persons file for the era in that case. I should warn you Miss that the outcome could turn out to be unpleasant.'

'Thank you inspector but I'm quite prepared for that. The whole thing is unpleasant,' she assured him.

'Quite. Well, thank you for your time Miss Harris.' The inspector blew out another smoke ring. 'Wells, you did inform Miss Harris that she could have the garden back didn't you?' he spun on his Sergeant like a puma.

'Yes Sir,'

'Good, good. Ok, I'll bid you goodnight Miss,' Inspector Allen plodded around the side of the house, the burnt out stub of his cigarette dangerously close to his lips, Sergeant Wells trotted after him like a faithful puppy.

Sophie watched them go then went inside to phone her mum.

The next evening Sophie sat in her lounge looking at the freshly painted walls and admiring Andy's handiwork. He had put the key back through the letterbox after he left and the room was perfect, all furniture back in its rightful place. A bunch of flowers lay on the dining table at the far end near the conservatory, with a little card pinned neatly to the cellophane.

For you Sophie, have a nice couple of days. I'll see you when I get back. Text me if you do change your number. I've asked Bill to come over later to start on the garden. We'll tackle the hall, landing and stairs when I get home. Take care, Andy.

P.S – mind the lounge walls, the paint may be tacky for a few hours.

xxx

Bill was digging over the garden outside in the fading sunlight. With the exception of offering a cup of tea, which he had declined, she had little to say to him. Nice though he seemed to be, he didn't seem the chatty type and preferred to get on with the digging.

'So, you've worked for Andy a while then?'

'Not long,' he told her, his eyes fixated on his task.

'Bet he's nice to work for,' she attempted. 'Seems very um…fair' she tried again.

'Yes,' Bill answered shortly.

125

'Right well, you're sure you don't want a cup of tea?' she asked again.

'I'm sure, thanks.'

'How about coffee then?' she sparked up.

'No, thanks,' Bill continued to dig without looking up.

She decided to leave him to it and ventured back inside. The patchwork scenery was not progressing as well as she had hoped and she had reluctantly agreed to take it home. It wasn't going to be finished in time otherwise.

Spread across the floor like a magic carpet she began placing the children's artwork into as tasteful an order as possible, then took out the needle and cotton. She was still sewing when the phone rang. Tucking it between her ear and her shoulder she continued to stitch but the gulps of gluey mess some of the children had created made it even more difficult to knit together.

'Hello,' she sang, pinching her finger for the forth time. 'Oww,' she winched.

'What have you done?' Linda asked

'Oh hiya,' she said, sucking her bleeding thumb. 'I'm doing the fete scenery but I've pricked my thumb with the needle.'

'Whatever you doing that at home for girl?'

'There isn't time. Anyway, you ok?'

'Yeah, just thought I'd give you a call. I've decided I'll take my maternity leave after the fete,' Linda announced. 'Little early but the head is a bit tetchy about my being there right up to the due date.'

'You don't say,' Sophie mocked. 'He's been tetchy about your being there since you announced you were pregnant. I bet he's secretly afraid of pregnant women,' Sophie giggled.

'Um yes, he has been avoiding me!'

'See, he's scared out of his wits that you'll go into labour in the middle of assembly!' Sophie rested the stitching and looked out through the conservatory where Bill was digging like a man possessed.

'I thought you had the dream boat there tonight anyway?'

'My "dreamboat" as you call him is away. Anyway, we've finished the painting, just the hall, stairs and landing to go. He's sent his assistant round tonight, he's out there digging over the garden for me.'

'Oh, is he gorgeous too?' Linda giggled heartily.

'Hardly, he's sixty!' Sophie declared. 'Besides, I thought we established that I couldn't have Andy since he's already attached, damn it.'

'Doesn't mean you can't look dear,' Linda scoffed. 'You can always look, even in my condition I can look!'

'And you do, I saw you checking out that behind on that alarm engineer yesterday!'

'Naturally, naturally,' Linda laughed. 'Good, nice and firm! Anyway, best go dear, I'll catch you tomorrow.'

'Righto, goodnight,' Sophie said. 'Sweet dreams!'

'You too dear, you too,' Linda giggled as she put the receiver down and Sophie listened to the click. Linda was right; she was ok to look. Trouble was she had gone past looking. The beautiful flowers that now stood proudly in a vase over the fireplace proved that. It wasn't fair, why did she have to appoint the most desirable DIY gardener in the county?

Why did she have to go and fall for him?

'Miss Harris?' a voice cut into her thoughts. Sophie visibly jumped.

'Sorry Miss Harris,' it was Bill, calling through the conservatory glass from the garden. She leapt to her feet and met him by the back door. 'Sorry, didn't want to get me muddy boots on ya nice clean floor,' his guff voice explained. Sophie thought this was the longest sentence she had heard him utter.

'Thank you,' she smiled. 'Did you want that tea now?'

'No thanks,' he told her resolutely. 'I wanted to give ya this,' he tossed a scruffy piece of paper into her hand and proceeded to remove his boots, hitting them hard against the patio to release the loose mud. Sophie flinched slightly at his strength. He was strong for a man of his years, stronger than he looked she thought.

'Thank you,' she said, unscrewing the paper as he waved a hand in the air and left around the side of the house, his boots in hand. She closed the door and went to spy on him getting into his van at the front. He slipped on some causal shoes, slung his boots into the back and drove away. He moved in a measured, somehow calculated way, his efforts completely un-wasted.

She unfolded the paper and took in a deep sigh. Whatever did he mean by sending her this?

I carry a cross in my pocket
A simple reminder to me
Of the fact that I am a Christian
No matter where I may be

This little cross isn't magic
Nor is it a good luck charm
It isn't meant to protect me
From every physical harm

It's not for identification
For all the world to see
It's simply an understanding
Between my saviour and me

When I put my hand in my pocket
To bring out a coin or a key
The cross is there to remind me
Of the price He paid for me

It reminds me too to be thankful
For my blessings day by day
And to strive to serve Him better
In all I do or say

It's also a daily reminder
Of the peace and comfort I share
With all who know my Master

128

And give themselves to His care

So I carry a cross in my pocket
Reminding no one but me
That Jesus Christ is Lord of my life
If only I'd let Him be.

Chapter Ten

June 1935 – Diary of Elise Harris

I wonder about Frederick. How selfish he is. How he wants me to be the moulded perfect wife for him without a life of my own. Tom would not do this to me. He never expects that of me, never asks me to do the impossible act of behaving as if everything is wonderful and that the world is lovely to me when in fact, it simply isn't. My world is far from ideal.

I feel like such an evil witch even to think this way but sadly it has come to this. Frederick makes me think this way. Forces my thoughts in the directions of self pity by his very absence, his neglect, his lack of care for me and his total indifference to my wants, my desires, my needs, me.

The real problem is that it doesn't even matter anymore if he does in truth still care for me, or if he wants this to work out happily forever. I don't love him anymore, maybe I never did. How can I be sure of exactly how I feel? And yet I know I love Tom with all my heart. I've loved him for a long time now; so long I can't even be sure when it started. It just crept up on me one day when my guard was down and now I can't stop it, I can't help myself. I want him to touch me, to love me and only me. I want him so much it hurts. My tears are relentless when I remember that he belongs to another. This is my punishment I have decided. To live with Frederick and to live in this loveless situation forever, my punishment for falling in love with one that is forbidden.

How unfair life can really be. I wonder how many lost souls are out there thinking the same as me? I take comfort in the fact that by sheer logic alone there must be thousands. At least in that I am not alone.

How many people are in the world thinking that they want something they know they can't have? Something they may never be able to obtain? How many people are dreaming every second of something that they know can never be theirs? How many people can understand just how cruel that really feels and how impossible it is to cope with? Yet cope with it I will. I plaster a smile on my face and take a deep breath. I move away from the window and go downstairs to keep company for Clarissa.

I am over the moon today. I can't stop smiling.

'It'll be ok my darling,' he told me yesterday, his voice like treacle down the static phone line. I softened at his assurances, I always do. This is the best thing that has ever happened to me and I know he feels it too. Frederick will survive without me. He has always been more in need of me than in love with me. He will easily replace me; he may even find someone his mother will approve of. I know it is unfair but the world is changing. We had a new prime minister, Stanley Baldwin just the other week. There are so many motorcars now that a speed limit has been introduced. I am so happy to be finally freeing myself from drudgery. I can't help but hum to *I'm in the Mood for Love* all day long. It is probably driving Clarissa crazy but I simply don't care anymore!

'I love you,' I told him, only the other day, my voice whispering from habit rather than necessity.

'I love you too,' he smiled. I could hear his smile, imagine the corners of his face; feel his skin beneath my fingers. There was nothing I couldn't imagine. I feel as if I have known him forever.

'I'll pick you up at 2.30. We can catch the 4 o'clock train.'

'How can I get the money for the ticket?' I panicked, my voice cracking under the strain of losing my dream.

'It's all right darling, I will get the tickets, both of them,' he told me.

'What about when we get there,' I whispered, 'where will we stay?'

'Perhaps you're right, we'd better book ahead, in case every hotel is full. I'll make the booking. Once we've got divorced we can marry my darling. We may only be able to secure a cook at first. We may even have to stay in rooms for the first month.'

'I don't mind, I really don't mind, anything that will allows us to be together,' I assured him.

'I'll get us a nice little house my love. They're building houses up north too darling, don't worry, it'll be fine.'

A pale hand picked up the receiver, covering the mouthpiece so they wouldn't hear the breathing down the line.

'I can't wait,' I told him, still whispering. 'I love you so much. It will be ok won't it?'

'Yes my darling,' he blew a kiss down the line and my whole body tingled with excitement of the future ahead of us. 'Don't worry about a thing. It'll be fine. When shall we go?' I smiled brightly. I don't think I've ever been happier.

'As soon as possible,' I whispered.

'Ok, I'll let you know once I've got us booked in somewhere. I have to go now sweetheart. I'll see you tomorrow,' he blew me another kiss.

'Tomorrow,' I whispered and replaced the receiver.

I went next door to see Albert & Katie today. I told them I was leaving. I couldn't just desert them. Not after all they have done for me. They have been so kind over the years. It is quite sad really but I think they are the only friends I've got.

'Welcome, welcome,' Albert's round face greeted me in the hall. Albert's hair is now a mass of grey but Katie told me it was once the same hazel shade as his eyes. He wore a grey jacket today with trousers and a pale green shirt. He smiled at me warmly and I noticed the wrinkles fade away with his sparkle. We went into the sitting room and Katie rang the bell for tea. Their parlourmaid appeared with a large silver tray, rested it on the central table as Katie indicated and left quietly. Albert was standing by the fireplace smoking his pipe.

'Hello my dear,' Katie said, 'how are you today? Isn't it a lovely day, I've just asked Hilda to put out the washing, should catch a lovely breeze in this sunshine,' she busied herself with cups, saucers, milk and sugar and rested the tea pot back on the tray.

I felt uneasy about the news but I knew it was the right thing to do. As it turned out I had nothing to fear.

'I wanted to tell you something,' I said, smiling to put them at ease. 'I, um, well…'

'I think I can guess my dear,' Katie said, her blue eyes were smiling at me as she took my hand in hers. Albert looked perplexed. I looked at her carefully. Did she know? Had she always known?

'Really?' I asked hesitantly. 'Do you think I'm wrong?' Katie only chuckled at me.

'He doesn't understand,' she laughed indicating Albert. 'Pour the tea love, will you?' she smiled at her husband who shook his head in bewilderment and got up to do as obliged. I have often wondered in years previous, before I met Tom of course, how they managed to look so happy by comparison to Frederick and I. It struck me that they were simply happy. How uniquely beautiful I thought. Now at last, it was finally my turn for happiness.

'You see I tend to notice things, you know, silly things, I suppose you would call it being nosy.' Katie squeezed my hand. 'I know you've never been in love with Frederick. 'He's not a bad man is he, but well, not what a woman really wants forever is it, to just settle for.' I almost cried with the relief. Someone had understood. Whyever hadn't I spoken to Katie before? 'So, when do you leave my dear?' Katie asked.

'I'm not sure exactly but it will be very soon,' I told her. 'I didn't want to go without saying goodbye.' Albert was still baffled. I smiled brightly at him. 'I'll miss you both,' I whispered, 'I know it looks bad but I love him.'

'Yes, I imagine you do my dear,' Katie said, 'he is very handsome isn't he. I saw the two of you in the town a couple of times,' she confessed, 'and I saw him leave your house a short while ago.' I must have looked concerned. 'Oh don't worry I never said a word, not even to Bert, have I love?' Katie's hair bobbed around her face as she spun a little to look at her husband behind her. She is a real lady, knows exactly what to wear, how to dress and how to behave. I really will miss her terribly. Just speaking to her daily over a cup of tea is wonderful. I hope I'll make new friends in the north. I'm not even sure exactly where we are headed, wherever Tom can find for us to reside I suppose, not that I care. It'll make little difference so long as we're together.

'Haven't the faintest idea what you're talking about ladies,' Albert said as he rejoined us by sitting and unsettled the tray of tea things with a slight clatter. 'I don't mean to pry, really I don't, but perhaps you could tell me what's going on?'

'I'm sure you don't Bert, my love. Elise here is eloping with her lover. She is leaving Frederick,' Katie told him, still holding my hand. 'Can you pour love?' she nodded at the still empty cups. Albert's face contorted into confusion. 'It's ok, Frederick doesn't know and when Elise has gone we'll go round there and comfort him. But we won't say we knew she was going. We'll just try to make him see that she wasn't happy,' Katie smiled at me. I felt wretched that I hadn't sought her comfort earlier in my life. How naïve of me to think she wouldn't have understood. How silly I have been.

'I don't know how to thank you,' I whispered. 'I'll write to you, once we're settled. I promise.'

'Oh I know you will my dear. I hope you'll both be happy together. Just one thing though my dear, you will be careful won't you? You're so close now, I would hate to see you endure Frederick's wrath if he finds out. We all know how bad his temper can be.'

'Yes, I know,' I sighed. 'Don't worry, I'll be careful. I promise,' I smiled again. I can't help smiling these days. If anything it'll be my smile that gives me away.

One day very soon I shall write from my new home, my new life with Thomas Brody, oh dear diary, you shall soon be filled with only glorious happy entries. The lonely empty years will soon be behind me. The future, my future with Tom, it stretches ahead of me like a dream, and this time, my dream is going to come true.

I wish I were leaving tomorrow, indeed I wish I had already left yesterday.

I laugh as I imagine their faces when they discover my absence! I shall write to Betsy via dear Katie. I will invite her to join us in the north once we are settled. Tom agreed this was a good plan.

Oh I can hardly sleep with the excitement of it all.

Chapter Eleven

April 2009

The doors swung open, letting in another blast of cold air that whirled around the atmosphere gathering strength from the scent of defeat. Sophie took a seat as instructed by the desk sergeant, as far away as possible from the man in the oversized woollen coat slumped in the corner. Momentarily he looked up at her as she sat down daintily. His eyes were the colour of deep green when he stared at her intently, and his face was crumpled far beyond all resemblance of the person he used to be. With a loud burp and a grin he fell back into his heap and Sophie averted her gaze. The desk sergeant sighed at the tramp and gave Sophie an apologetic smile.

'See the charming house guests we get in here,' he said casually, turning to pick up the ringing phone. 'Sergeant Wells will be with you in a minute,' he said reassuringly and answered the phone. 'Good morning…'

The man's belch left a stench of stale beer, cigarettes and dead fish. Sophie willed the doors to swing open again just for the whish of coldness to purify the air. He was shuffling nosily in his seat, angry in his half-comatose state.

Sophie looked around the station. Varying closed doors presented themselves as possible escape routes away from the drunken tramp in reception, each with the challenge of cracking the number lock before entry could be permitted. She examined her finger nails for want of anything better to do and wondered how long she would have to wait.

The tramp fidgeted in his uncomfortable seat and shuffled along a couple closer to her. She sat motionless, praying she wouldn't be forced to demonstrate sheer rudeness by selecting another seat herself.

The inspector wanted to see her apparently, so Wells had told her on the phone. They had identified the male remains and wanted her collaboration. What use she would be was beyond her contemplation; hadn't she already told him that she knew nothing of the family before her grandmother, and even less about their friends and associates.

'Miss Harris,' Sergeant Wells appeared like a vision in one of the doorways.

Sophie leapt to her feet.

'Sergeant,' she cried in relief as the tramp shuffled even further along the row of plastic chairs.

'This way Miss,' Sergeant Wells held the door for her as she followed him along the maze of corridors and closed doors. 'Inspector Allen is in here,' he held open a door to an untidy office. The faintness of dying smoke rings protruded over a stack of buff coloured files on a desk. The air wasn't much better than reception she decided, taking a seat in the opposite chair as indicated by the sergeant. Inspector Allen mumbled something to Wells who swiftly collected the enormous stack of files and dumped them unceremoniously on his own laden desk in the corner of the room. He perched on the edge crossing his ankles and waited.

Inspector Allen was busy stubbing his cigarette out in an over-flowing ashtray hidden in his desk drawer. He smiled at Sophie briefly as he picked up a slim file.

'Thank you for coming in Miss Harris. Wells and I have been up all night going through the missing persons file for 1935 haven't we son?' Wells nodded silently. 'We think we've managed to identify the male remains as Tom Brody.' Inspector Allen handed her a black and white photo. Sophie looked at Thomas Brody; his piercing eyes almost transfixed her even from the photograph. He had fair hair and seemed quite tall. Sophie looked into the handsome face. Was this really the man buried next to Elise in her garden?

'Thomas Brody,' read the inspector from the case file notes now in his hand. 'Aged 42, married to a Cheryl Brody,

137

6ft 2, blond hair, blue eyes, gentleman with private income at the time of his disappearance in November 1935, reported missing by his wife just after Christmas. She came in to report his absence in the new year of 1936.'

'So you think this is the man found in my garden?' Sophie traced the outline of the man's face with her fingertips.

'The name doesn't mean anything to you?'

'No, like I said, I don't know the family that far back,' she answered without looking up. 'His death isn't recorded then?'

'No. According to the records he is still alive, which can't possibly be true given his age at the time of his disappearance. This is all we have to go on,' Inspector Allen said, indicating the missing persons report in his hand. 'And this,' he said, reaching for a note pinned to the inside cover of the file.

Sophie read the note twice.

Mrs Cheryl Brody reported her husband missing this evening Sarge, but I got a funny feeling about it; she didn't seem all that concerned, quite keen to get back outside to her friend. She was in a fancy motorcar. All dolled up she was like she was going out for the evening. I don't know, it's just a feeling that she knew he wasn't coming back and cared even less. I told her we would look into it, made her fill in the report. When she drove away I watched her and her friend in the fancy motorcar, because I would like one of them cars like myself, and they was drinking champagne. Like I said, just a feeling but she didn't look very worried about her husband to me. I have got the late shift tomorrow Sarge, see you later

PC Stringer

'That's odd,' Sophie said handing the note back to the inspector who was toying with his cigarettes, clearly keen to light up despite the no smoking notice on the wall behind his head.

Inspector Allen nodded gravely.

'Can you actually confirm that the skeleton is this Thomas Brody?' she asked him. The inspector nodded again.

'Yep, we can confirm it all right; it was definitely him. Back then we didn't have DNA but our forensics team today are pretty smart. When he was missing they fished around his house a bit, it was a routine thing, and our forensics team can match something from the evidence box with the DNA on the bones. Don't ask me how, they're real smart in that lab.'

'Wow,' Sophie said 'so that's it, the case is closed?'

'Yep, that's it. I just thought you'd like to know before the story hits the papers. The real link between Elise Harris and Thomas Brody will probably be a mystery for all of time but you can guess the obvious one; that'll be the one the tabloids go with.'

'I see, thank you Inspector. What about the notes I've been getting?'

'Well we're still working on that Miss Harris. There are no fingerprints on the envelopes or the notes themselves. The letters are stuck down with super glue, and they come from very recent newspapers, but that's about all I can tell you for the moment. Have you received any more?'

'No,' she sighed. 'Do you think they'll stop now that the case is solved?'

'I hope so Miss Harris, I really do,' the inspector fingered his cigarettes with growing interest. He leant forward on the desk and Sophie could smell his breath, vile from the tobacco. 'I do hope so but you know where we are if they become more threatening. We'll try to keep the story from the tabloids but you know it may be better if it makes the press. That way whoever is sending you this filth will know it's over and there'll be no reason left to write to you. It is intriguing though, the notion that someone out there today knows about this case. I mean, it has to be someone very very old…' The inspector sat back in his chair and rocked on the back legs.

'Or a descendent of the original killer,' piped up Wells. Sophie and the inspector turned towards him quickly.

'Yes yes, I hadn't thought of that son, perhaps you could look into that for us this afternoon.'

'You mean find the killer of over seventy years ago?' Wells looked sceptical. Inspector Allen smiled at him and returned to Sophie, his cigarette perched back into his mouth.

'Don't worry Miss,' he looked at her and puffed out an imaginary long stream of smoke. 'We'll get on to it. That's all

Miss for now I think, thanks for coming in. Son, see Miss Harris out will you.'

The children were running wildly about the playground when Sophie entered the school gates, an hour or so later than usual due to her summons to the police station.

'Ha, good morning Sophie my dear, how did you get on this morning?' the headmaster clung to the edges of his forest green tank top as he spoke to her, his glasses perched on the end of his nose.

'Fine, thank you,' she smiled. 'Sorry about the short notice.'

'Not a problem my dear, not a problem.' Even outside he rocked slightly on his heels. 'I wanted to have a word with you my dear about Linda.'

'Yes?'

'Well she'll be taking leave soon I expect and I er, wondered, if you'd take on some of her classes? You see we can't afford to take on another full time person to cover work so I was hoping that between you and Pat we could manage. What'd you say my dear?'

'Oh well, yes but...'

'Splendid, I knew I could count on you my dear,' he looked delighted, patted her on the arm and glanced over her head sharply. 'Oh Billy, no, don't do that,' he cried after one of the children and was gone, his heel rocking giving him momentum to semi-sprint across the playground towards a couple of six year old boys arguing over a football.

Sophie discarded her bags and books on her desk heavily and sat down behind the desk wearily. The day felt long already and the first playtime was barely behind her. At least there was no rehearsal tonight she thought as she prepared her notes for the next lesson. The substitute teacher had been in whilst she'd been at the police station and the desk was a mess. Swiftly she piled up the substitute's belongings and laid out her lesson plan for literacy hour. A nice quiet lesson, she thought, they can read a little and write stories about their weekends.

The children came into the room like an explosion. Nosily they took their seats and squabbled over pencil cases.

'Quiet!' she cried, 'now children, good morning, we're about to start so please quieten down and take out your notebooks and pencils.' She tapped into the laptop and the words sprung up on the projector screen *what I did at the weekend* and turned to face the class.

'First we're going to read this short story and then you're going to write about what you did at the weekend. Jimmy, please stop that!' The boy took the eraser out of his mouth sullenly.

'Jimmy you can start us off. Read from page one of *Clara's Playtime*.' Sophie rubbed her temples as the children read, pronouncing each word's every syllable with clarity. When the story was over she sat behind her desk. 'Now then, I want you each to write about your weekend in your notebooks. Start with when you finished school on Friday and finish with coming to school on Monday morning,' she told them. A ruffle of papers and scratching of pencils filled the otherwise silent air as she took out a stack of marking and her red pen.

'Miss?'

'Yes Charlotte?'

'How do you spell Daddy's house?'

Sophie spelt out the words slowly as Charlotte noted them down.

'I went to Daddy's house too on Sunday,' Annabel told Charlotte proudly. 'He made me a coke float, it was lovely!' Sophie jolted her head up to Annabel. Her Daddy's house... did that mean her beloved daddy wasn't living with her and her mother?

'What's a coke float?' Charlotte enquired as the rest of the room began to listen in. Sophie sat glued to her seat, unable to interrupt the young conversation.

'You put ice cream in the bottom of a really tall glass and then you put coke cola over it and it all fizzes up!' giggled Annabel. 'It's lovely,'

'I'm going to ask my Daddy to do that,' Charlotte declared.

'Me too,' Jimmy said. 'Can you have chocolate ice cream?'

'Yes, and vanilla, and strawberry and…'

'Miss?'

'Yes Jimmy?'

'Why do other Mummies and Daddies live in different houses? Mine live in the same house, with me,' he sat chewing the end of his pencil.

'Take the pencil out of your mouth Jimmy or you'll get lead poisoning. Some mums and dads decide they'd like to live in different houses; that's all. They still love you the same, they just get along with each other better if they don't live together. You're lucky Jimmy, your mummy and daddy have decided they like to live in the same house but not everybody is the same.'

'Why?' Annabel asked.

'There are lots of reasons Annabel,' Sophie told her, wondering again if she had completely misread the situation.

'My daddy lives in two houses,' she said, 'sometimes he sleeps in my house and sometimes he sleeps in another house.'

'Really?' Sophie asked her leaning forward over her desk. *Get a grip* she told herself. *You cannot question his daughter like this.*

'Yes, sometimes he sleeps in my house, and I sometimes sleep in his house,' she said proudly. 'I have two bedrooms,' she beamed.

'So do I,' said Charlotte defensively clutching her pencil.

'Ok children, ok, that's enough. Annabel, why don't you write about your coke float. Quiet now so you'll be able to concentrate. Shss…' she put her fingers to her lips.

Why would he have two homes…? Had she completely misunderstood? Was there a chance after all…? A shimmer of hope mingled with fear flushed through her body and she didn't know whether or cry or laugh. *Get a grip*.

Sophie parked her car in the driveway and beeped it locked. Glad to be home she unlocked the front door, trod over the post and sauntered through to the kitchen. To her surprise

Bill was already in the garden, the digging commenced. He must have let himself round the side, she thought. Not that it was a problem but perhaps she'd get a lock for the side gate. She opened the window and leant out over the sink.

'Hi Bill, do you want a cuppa?'

Bill put a hand on the small of his back and rose upright with a wave and nod of his head. Sophie watched him stretch out for a moment and wondered if he was really up to the job. He wasn't a young man. Did Andy know he suffered with backache? It was none of her business was it; she thought, as she flicked the kettle on and pulled out two mugs from the cupboard.

She had decided not to mention the note he had given her last time. Perhaps it was an innocent mistake and he meant to leave her the invoice for the work. It was a shaky notion admittedly, but feasible. Either way, she wasn't going to ask him about it.

Taking off her coat and shoes she slung them in the hallway. The post lay on the doormat ominously. The cream envelope looked uninviting. She gave out a little cry. Not another one, please not another one, she picked up the other business letters and fetched a plastic food bag from the kitchen. With the bag inside out she managed to contain the incriminating letter within the plastic bag without touching it and tied a knot in the end. She didn't even want to read it. With spite she cast it aside on the telephone table in the hallway and dialled the police station. They agreed to send someone to pick it up later that evening.

When the policeman arrived he slid on a pair of white gloves and opened the letter.

SO YOU'VE GOT A SUBSTITUTE HAVE YOU? HOW NICE, A BIT OF COMPANY FOR YOU WHILEST LOVER BOY IS AWAY. IS HE STAYING AWAY FOR LONG THEN? DON'T BET ON HIS RETURN ANY TIME SOON GIRL, A PRIME TARGET FOR ME TO MAKE A POINT. I TOLD YOU BEFORE, YOU HAVEN'T LISTENED TO ME AND I'VE WARNED YOU ABOUT WHAT MIGHT HAPPEN IF I GET

ANGRY. YOU REALLY DON'T WANT TO SEE THAT, BUT IF YOU INSIST YOU'VE GOT IT! WATCH YOUR BACK AND TELL LOVERBOY TO WATCH HIS AN'ALL!

The letter and envelope plopped into an official police evidence bag and the police constable was gone. Sophie sighed as she locked and bolted the door behind him. Bill hadn't seen anyone, the police had questioned him about his arrival time but he swore he hadn't seen another soul.

'God bless my dear,' he had said, packed up his tools and left. Sophie watched after him as he drove away down the road; a nice old man she thought, probably just concerned for her. Pity that the younger generations, despite her best efforts each day at school, cared so much less about others than their elders.

She took a glass of wine into the lounge and flicked on the TV. Distraction. That was what she needed, distraction and wine.

Linda was wedged into Glenis's favourite chair, her stomach kicking riotously. Sophie brought the coffees over and took a seat next to her.

'I reckon it's going to be a footballer, here,' Linda took Sophie's hand 'feel.'

'Striker I'd say,' Sophie smiled. 'Does it hurt?' Linda shook her head and sipped her coffee.

'Nah, only when it scores!' she smiled.

'Have you thought of any names yet?' Sophie asked, noticing a seriously displeased Glenis eyeing up her chair.

'Oh yeah, well Paul wants Alex for a boy and Delia for a girl. I've told him no on both counts!' Sophie laughed. It would be Linda who won the argument. It was always Linda who won. Poor Paul. 'I fancy something more exotic.'

'Such as?'

'I don't know, how about Alexia – that's not far off Alex.'

'Yeah but didn't he want Alex for a boy? Alexia is a girl's name surely?'

144

'See how I compromise,' Linda smirked. 'We said we'd wait until the baby was here to name it,' she explained. 'I don't mind his choices actually but don't tell him I said so!' she giggled. 'Let them sweat honey, always let them sweat,' she drank more coffee. 'I can't have another cup today' she said, 'I'm already on the borderline. God, I can't wait to have unlimited tea and coffee again. Fruit tea just isn't the same,' she declared draining the last of her coffee and clanging it down on the table.

'Um, I imagine not,' Sophie agreed. The staff room was filling up as the other teachers stood in little groups, chatting about the latest antics of the Hooper boy in year three. 'How's the blood pressure?' Sophie asked, not wanting Linda to hear about Hooper since he'd be in her next class.

'Never better. Apparently being pregnant now suits my blood pressure just fine so at least I have a cure at last!' she laughed again. 'How are things with you?'

'Better,' Sophie said quietly. 'The case is solved now, did I tell you?'

Linda looked incredulous. 'No woman you did not, out with it. Who was the mystery killer of the pre-war years then?'

'Well, not that solved,' Sophie smiled, drank more coffee and wondered where to begin. 'They've identified the victims and the cause of death, that's all. Little point in searching for a killer who is probably dead after all this time.'

'Still, justice should be done,' Linda wagged her finger. 'Who were they then, those poor souls beneath the daisies?'

'My great great aunt Elise, she was married to my great great grandfather's brother. And some guy called Thomas Brody but we haven't the foggiest idea who he was!' Sophie finished her coffee and piled it on top of Linda's empty mug. Cathy, the caretaker would be round shortly to clear up after the teachers. She always came in tutting and sighing after every break.

'Doesn't sound very solved to me,' Linda quipped, 'seems they've only named them. How'd they die, it wasn't some national plague or disease was it? Be fitting just to bury them in the garden if it was a national crisis; graveyards were probably bursting at the seams.'

Sophie laughed at her.

'Just because it was before the second world war doesn't mean they were pre-historic you know,' she giggled. 'I reckon they had a good life all in all. I mean the war hadn't started so they hadn't gone onto food rations or anything like that. They were pretty happy I should imagine, none of these computer games or back-chatting children we get now.'

'Except those poor souls who managed to get themselves killed,' Linda pointed out. 'What was the cause of death then?' The antics of the Hooper boy had vanished to a far corner, much to Sophie's relief. It would be the boy's fault if he pulled a fast one on Linda, with her hormones all over the place he didn't stand a chance. She had probably done him a favour and given him a head start.

'Stabbed,' Sophie said, enjoying the look of shock on Linda's face. 'Through the heart, both of them.'

'Oh my God! Why?'

'Who knows! Thomas Brody was reported missing by his wife but Elise wasn't. Frederick must have wondered where she'd gone but she wasn't reported missing and she never died – at least there isn't a death certificate for her, nor for Thomas Brody.'

'Do you think Frederick did her in then?' Linda looked hideously excited.

Sophie felt the colour drain from her face and a faintness sweep over her. Linda was right, Frederick was the most likely suspect...her worst fears of the murderer being a member of her family had finally hit home.

'It hadn't...hadn't...I hadn't thought of that,' she whispered. All this time she had been feeling better that the police hadn't incriminated her own family when surely they were thinking the same as Linda. It was always the spouse wasn't it...almost every time.

'Hey, hey, don't worry honey. I didn't mean it, honest. It was probably a break-in gone wrong or something. You ok?' Linda took Sophie's hand and was tapping it quite hard. 'I'm sorry,' she stumbled, backtracking but it was too late. The obvious solution was probably the right one and Sophie knew it.

There was a real murderer in her family tree.

Sophie spent the rest of the day in a kind of daze. She fudged her way through one class after another until the bell sounded and she packed up her books and sat in her car, taking a deep breath before driving home. It couldn't be. It just couldn't be true. She would ring the police station she decided, taking a left when she actually wanted a right at the roundabout. She would ring and ask them to pursue the case until they could categorically prove that the murderer wasn't a member of her own flesh and blood.

Beep, beep, beep

The car horn of the red mazda made her jump. She waved politely at the other driver and moved off. The traffic lights were green. *Get a grip, get a grip* she chanted all the way home.

Picking up the receiver she heard a voice.

'Hello?'

'Hi Sophie. It's only Andy. Were you sitting on the phone? It didn't even ring!' he laughed.

'I was about to dial out,' she said, her own voice sounding flat.

'What's wrong? You sound different.'

'It's nothing, I heard back from the police that's all. How are you?' she tried to sound brighter but Andy wasn't fooled.

'What did they say?'

'They said the skeletons were Elise Harris, my great great aunt and a man called Thomas Brody,' she explained. 'Both stabbed but they can't say who by,' she said without feeling. 'So, how are you?'

'I'm fine, but you're not are you. Have you received another note or something?' Andy's voice sounded strong. If only he were with her, holding her. It would all seem better. But he wasn't and she knew she would have to manage alone.

'Oh yes, I got one of those too.' She could hear the distance in her own voice. 'I've given it to the police already.'

'Are they doing anything about it?' he wanted to know but she couldn't answer him. 'I got your text,' he said when she remained silent. 'Thanks for the new number.'

'You're welcome,' she whispered. 'How did it go with your meeting?'

'I got it! Thanks to you, that reference was superb,' he said, 'thanks so much Soph. It'll make a huge difference to the firm. How is Bill getting on?'

'Oh he's doing ok,' she thought about his backache and his weird message to her. 'Fine,' she confirmed. 'Almost done with the digging I think,' she added straining to see through the hallway into the kitchen and out the window. As far as she could tell Bill wasn't there today.

'I'll be home tomorrow,' Andy told her, 'looking forward to seeing you again Soph, I'd better go though, the signal isn't too great and my battery is getting low.'

'Ok, see you when you get back,' she said, 'goodnight.'

'Goodnight Soph,' he said, 'listen, don't worry ok, I'll be back as soon as I can.' Sophie nodded in response and put the telephone down numbly. She wandered into the kitchen and peered out the window but Bill was not there.

The water was hot. The whisps of fragrance filtered from the lavender bath oil as she poured it under the running steam. Soft music floated in from the bedroom and candles adorned the edge of the bath.

Sophie dipped her toes into the water and sank quickly into the depths of relaxation. It was all too much; the skeletons in her garden, the possibility that a murderer lurked in her family tree, the notes from the poison pen threatening to murder her in her sleep, the rather odd Bill digging over the garden, the summer fete was in two days time, Linda would start her maternity leave and she would have to take on extra classes, then there was Andy. He was really the crux of her emotional nightmare. Was he single or wasn't he?

I'll ask him, outright, once and for all she thought. *I'll just ask him. We're both adults, we both know what's been going on.* She sighed. *I can't do that!* She cried helplessly to herself, closed her eyes and sank lower into the bubbles.

Roll on another day she whispered. Maybe it'll all become clearer.

28th April 2009   Issue No 2050

ATWOOD CHRONICLE

Cause of Buried Deaths Confirmed

The cause of death for the two bodies found locally buried in a private garden has been confirmed. Both victims, Elise Harris and Thomas Brody, died from stab wounds to the chest, one of two blows, the other with one fatal strike. Each body will be reunited with family members as soon as possible, but testing is still continuing to establish as much evidence as possible to source the identity of the killer. It is thought that the same killer is responsible for both deaths.

Furthermore it is discovered that both parties were married, but not to each other! This discovery brings questions to the surface of why a missing persons report wasn't filed at the time for one of the two victims.

Murder is a certainty in these cases now, as police strive to unearth the answers that, as yet, defy us all. The investigation continues but the connection between both dead bodies now seems to have an obvious conclusion.

We'll keep you posted.

Chapter Twelve

15th July 1935 – Diary of Elise Harris

Today Tom called and told me Cheryl is refusing to grant him a divorce. He said we would elope anyway. I know it's wrong, I shouldn't agree to go and live with a man when we can't be married – at least not straight away. She will have to agree eventually. I haven't even told Frederick yet; he may refuse to divorce me too. What a mess. I know it's wrong but I want so much to be with Tom. We said we would still go. Oh, how much I want to go...

Tom said he hadn't intended to tell her but she found out. The evil witch had been listening in to our telephone conversations. Such appalling behaviour, even if I say so myself. Hypocritical I know, but she doesn't really love him, not like I do and Frederick doesn't love me, not like Tom does. We are going. I am so glad she has not managed to spoil things for us.

I'm worried though, worried she will tell Frederick before I can. He may be difficult, make it impossible for me to get away. What will I do if she goes to him before I can? Maybe I should tell him first... Oh I don't know. I will just sit tight and pray. Please God make it all ok. Please, please, please...

Flashback - November 1935

The day has come and I open the front door to see him standing there. He wears a blue shirt, the black jacket and tie I bought for him a few months ago. It's cold outside and I widen

150

the door to allow him entry. I close the door and we stand in the hallway, his suitcase now on the floor and our bodies pressed close together, his arms wrapped around me like a blanket. I close my eyes and he leans down to kiss me. His lips are soft on mine and I already feel as if the world is a better place.

Clarissa is out taking tea and Frederick is at his club. Last night I dared to tell Betsy and she wished us well. She promised to keep the staff out of sight this afternoon; some assistance was much needed in the soup kitchen for the needy in the town. It would demand their full attention until four o'clock had safely passed and was by way of a favour to Betsy whose own family were associated with its running.

'It's finally happening,' I say, a bright smile refusing to hide itself. He grins at me like a little boy and we mount the stairs to retrieve my things.

'How long until we have to leave for the train?' I ask him, my voice cracked with excitement.

'About half hour,' he says, his hands stroking my bottom as he follows me up the staircase. 'Just enough time,' he tells me, his voice sultry, 'to hold us until we arrive.' I smile at him and he leads me towards the bedroom. Ordinarily I would not allow this room, this house, but it seems pointless to hold onto such thoughts as we'll be leaving our lives and everyone in them behind us in twenty-nine minutes time. I can almost count the seconds.

With ease he picks my two suitcases from the bed and rests them outside the bedroom door, takes me into his embrace and softens his lips against me. My heartbeat quickens with the rush, the anticipation of a life we have wanted for so long, waited patiently for, prayed for. He sits on the edge of the bed, pulls me towards him, his legs encasing me so I'm pressed up close to him. I close my eyes and allow him the freedom I can't deny him. His fingers are cold as they brush aside my flimsy blouse and grace across my skin. He kisses me and I clutch at his shirt stretching across the top of his back. After another kiss I find myself on the bed. I giggle as he climbs

151

onto the bed at my feet, crawls over me and inclines his head once more, his lips destined for mine.

'How did you do that?' I whisper as he begins to unwrap me from my blouse, one button at a time, his eyes never leaving mine. 'That was very smooth' I say, my breath coming in short gasps.

'I spun you round,' he confesses, his grin widening broadly. 'I was quite impressed with myself too,' he grins some more as my blouse gives up its claim on me completely.

Our dreamy encounter is sharply interrupted with the sound of breaking glass. Tom looks at me with this piercing stare and I know not to make a sound. He creeps up from the bed and tiptoes over the floorboards towards the bedroom door. I lie motionless on the bed struggling to comprehend what might be happening. Frederick isn't due home for hours; he can't be home yet. Why would he break glass anyway, he has a key in the event that the staff are out…my confused mind scrambles on without reaching anything conclusive. My heart is racing. I lay on the bed, frightened for Tom. He doesn't know where the squeaky floorboards are, the ones to avoid when trying to be quiet. Any second now, yes, there it is. The creaking board near the door gives our presence away.

Another smash of broken glass erupts into our silent room, footsteps smashing it into tiny crumbs. Tom looks at me, his face the picture of broken hope. He signals for me to get up and I do so, quickly, buttoning my blouse hastily so some are wrong and I cannot force the last button into any of the holes. I feel the fear running through my veins and I feel the grief, the loss of our life we so very nearly got to have for ourselves. At best this is a burglar who may just run off when Tom spies him. We may miss the train now and if we are really unlucky we will lose our hotel booking at the other end as a result. At worst, we are in grave danger. I feel as if it's the latter and I'm suddenly afraid.

'Tom, no,' I whisper as loud as I dare. He spins to face me, puts his fingers to his mouth to hush me and I shake my head at him. 'No,' I mouth silently and tiptoe over the boards expertly, without a sound, reaching his side and grabbing his arm as he reaches for the door handle. The footsteps are getting louder. The intruder is mounting the stairs, one by one, loudly and without a care it seems.

Tom pushes me behind him. Even in this ridiculous situation he is trying to protect me and I begin to pray, hoping to God that my lack of faith all these years can be made up for now by the severity of my desire for us to escape. Moments linger as we stand, the vibration of fear so great I am sure he can feel me shaking. He grips my hands around his body. I feel his fear too as we wait for the inevitable to descend upon us.

The intruder has reached the top of the stairs, is pacing about the landing, chooses the far door and enters the back bedroom. Hastily we make a dash for it, almost slide down the stairs and fall into the hallway. The intruder sprints to catch us. Tom has the front door open, is about to shove me outside but it slams before my face and I feel Tom pulling me back into him, to widen the space and re-open the door.

I begin to scream now that our presence is no longer a secret. I don't realise I am crying until Tom pulls me towards the stairs, shoves me up a couple of steps and attempts to barricade himself between me and the intruder. I scream again as a silver reflection glistens in the sun beam that is now flooding the lounge from the front window. A knife. I almost faint with fright and I hear Tom's breathing – fast and heavy. Within a split second Tom has been dragged away from me and I scream for him, I call his name, I try to move, my feet feel like lead weights. It's too much, I'm completely confused, what should I do? Tom is shouting from the other room.

'No, don't do it, no, no, don't be stupid' he is saying. He isn't hurt at the moment. Whilst I hear his voice he isn't hurt. A bolt of sense strikes me and I aim for the kitchen where there is a telephone. I clutch at the receiver, begin to dial 99… A hand covers my mouth and I open it to scream but nothing comes out. The telephone is ripped from my grasp and I wrestle with my attacker as they drag me towards the sitting room.

I didn't see it coming. The pain is sudden and sharp, deep and more than I can bear. It's all I can do to keep my eyes open. They suddenly feel so heavy, the lids fluttering helplessly. My attacker lets go of me and I fall like a rock.

I hear the thump of my own body as I hit the floor. I hear my own scream fading into silence. I can smell blood. My breath is all but stopped; it is caught in my throat. All I see is a blurry vision of Tom's wide open mouth, his hand stretching out to save me and then...

Chapter Thirteen

April 2009

Sophie opened her eyes on Saturday morning to bright sunlight flooding in through the curtains. A nice day for the summer fete she thought. A loud clanking of metal on concrete made her jump. Outside she spied Andy and Bill unloading the van and trailing things around the side gate towards the garden. They were early.

She brushed her teeth, flashed into the shower, washed and dried her hair and threw on a pair of faded jeans and a casual purple top. It was Saturday and she didn't need to change into teacher mode until 2pm. It was only eight-thirty.

Downstairs she flicked on the kettle and opened the kitchen window.

'Hey, morning,' Andy called, his lean body wrapped in another tight t-shirt, legs clad in black jeans mildly splattered with white emulsion.

'Hi,' she whispered, aware her words were lost in the breeze. 'Do you want tea?' she called. Both men nodded gratefully. Bill was unwinding a cord from a contraption she had never seen before as Andy approached the window, his hands resting on the inside of the sill. She bought her face close to his and looked into his eyes. 'You came back,' she said.

'Couldn't stay away,' he winked at her. 'We've only got a couple of hours though this morning,' he said, 'as have you I suppose.'

'Yes, I have to be at the school by 2pm.'

'Likewise,' he beamed. 'I'll get Bill started,' he said, 'then I'll pop in and we can discuss the stairs and landing paint colours.' He winked at her again and strode across the expanse of green towards Bill.

Sophie watched Bill avoid her gaze. The religious reading sprang into her mind and she wondered, again, what he had meant. Eyeing him sceptically she contemplated giving it to Andy. Bill couldn't go round preaching at the customers, if indeed that was anywhere close to what he meant. Perhaps he meant to keep her safe in his own very feeble way...safe from what? Had Andy told him about the threatening letters?

It was a fruitless exercise; no further thoughts of any significance had emerged the longer she thought about it. In conclusion she had to admit that it meant nothing. There were things to do; she shoved it from her mind.

Sophie poured out three mugs of tea and took the two outside to Bill and Andy.

'So, how far do you think you'll get today then?' she asked. Bill grunted with the effort. Upon Andy's glance he afforded her a half smile.

'Almost finished probably,' he muffled into his spade as he sunk it deeper into the earth again.

'Thanks Bill,' Andy said. 'I'll just be showing Miss Harris the colour charts for the hallway and then I'll pop back out to give you a hand,' he said, his hand on the small of her back leading her towards the house. 'Let's go inside,' he suggested.

'You're in charge,' she mocked as they entered the kitchen. 'But I warn you, I must finish that scenery otherwise the play will not have a background!'

'Can I help?'

'Can you sow?' she teased, collecting her tea from the counter and leading the way towards the lounge. The final touches to the patchwork scenery would wait no longer, sprawled out as they were on the living room carpet. As she passed the doormat she noticed the post. It was rather early, usually it was nearer lunchtime...almost dropping her mug she managed to rest it on the telephone table and went in search of another plastic food bag from the kitchen. Just as she deposited it into the bag Andy came into the hallway.

'Hello,' he said into his mobile. 'Yes I'm at Sophie Harris's house, she has another threatening note, can you send someone round pl...yes, I'll stay with her...thank you.' He dropped the mobile and threw his arms around her, the plastic bag now on the telephone table.

'Ssh...they're sending a constable to collect it,' Andy said. 'Come on, let's go into the lounge.'

The constable opened the letter and slid it into another police evidence bag.

SO YOU KNOW WHO THE SKELETONS WERE – POOR STUPID VICTIMS – DO YOU THINK THEY KNEW WHAT THEY WERE GETTING INTO? HAVE YOU SOLVED THE MYSTERY YET? WHO DO YOU THINK MURDERED THEM IN COLD BLOOD? MAYBE YOUR KILLER HAS DESCENDENTS, EVENR THOUGHT OF THAT MY DEAR? HEY, DON'T WORRY TOO MUCH, THEY WERE JUST AN APPERTISER. THE MAIN COURSE IS STILL TO COME...

The summer fete was going well, there was the usual hustle and bustle of parents waving coats and bags and all sorts of paraphernalia around the hall. The children were running about, amongst the chairs set up for the play and in and out the stalls of icing covered biscuits, name the bear, guess the number of sweets in the jar and tiddlywinks, all raising money for a local hospice.

The jumble sale was selling out of junk and the cakes were a roaring success. The bouncy castle in the playground was proving very popular and most children were still without shoes.

Sophie was attaching the patchwork scenery with difficulty to the sports equipment on the wall at the back of the stage. String and bluetac were only going so far.

'Hey you, how's it coming?' Linda called up to Sophie.

'Could be better,' she called down. 'Do you have any sellotape?' Linda scuttled away and returned with the tape. 'You're a lifesaver,' she called, catching the reel as Linda tossed it up to her on the top rung of the ladder. She stuck large chunks of tape over all her dubious looking fixings and began to descend. 'Thanks,' she said, climbing down to the stage and leaping off to the floor where Linda stood looking up at the patchwork of drawings.

'You know that's not half bad,' Linda admired it. Sophie looked up at it. Linda was right, who would have thought it after all her finger pricking and cursing the thing looked good.

'Head wants me to take on some of your classes,' she told Linda, 'whilst you're off. Can you give me any tips? Who's bad, who's good, you know the sort of thing.'

'Sure, pop round one evening next week. My last day is Wednesday,' Linda smiled. 'So, you ready for the play?'

'If the children ever arrive yes, I haven't seen any of them yet.'

'Oh Annabel is here, I saw her with her parents just a moment ago,' Linda scanned the room. Sophie busied herself with removing the ladder. It was going to be a hard enough afternoon without the strife of seeing Andy with his arm around his wife.

'What about the others,' she called from the back corner; where she propped up the ladder out of sight. Perhaps she could focus on Jimmy and his disgusting habits instead.

'There she is,' Linda said stabbing a finger out towards a girl Sophie had hardly seen before. Sophie looked confused at Linda.

'No, that's not Annabel,' she said, 'she's...there,' her voice died on her as she spied Andy and Annabel entering the hall. Linda looked at Sophie as if she were mad.

'Oh, that Annabel, I thought you meant Annabel Taylor, the chubby girl over there eating a chocolate éclair?' Linda looked at Sophie again who was now fixated on Andy in the doorway.

'No, that's Andy Taylor see, just coming in through the main doors with his daughter Annabel...' Sophie whispered, her eyes still firmly on Andy.

'Yeah, his daughter is Annabel Weston. The little girl took her mother's name. I thought you meant the other Annabel; we have two my dear, both in my class, makes life very confusing at times I can tell you. Annabel Taylor as in Mr and Mrs Taylor...' Linda babbled on.

'You mean you thought I was talking about Mr Edward Taylor?' Sophie's eyes sparkled.

'I don't know his first name!' Linda cried, 'all you said was Taylor with a daughter called Annabel and that's Mr and Mrs Taylor over there with their daughter Annabel Taylor!'

'Oh my God! So you didn't mean Andy?'

'No, I don't really know Annabel Weston's father, I only ever see her mother; she's on her second marriage to Tony Weston. Come to think of it I don't even know her father's surname...'

Sophie felt like dancing. So Andy wasn't married...oh wait a minute she thought, how come his daughter said he spent some nights at her house? That didn't make any sense especially if Annabel's mother was married to Tony Weston.

'Everyone please, can I have your attention for a moment,' the headmaster's booming voice sounded over like a commentary. 'We're going to have our spectacular play now if you'd all like to take a seat. Would our actors and actresses go over there to Miss Harris please; and if our delightful choir could join Mr Ingles.' A chorus of postman pat started up. Linda approached the kids in question and silenced them most threatening with her large bump.

The children scurried along like mice and the parents fumbled with coats and shoes as they squeezed into the little chairs all facing the stage. Sophie could barely take her eyes off Andy. He was kissing his daughter on the forehead and whispering something in her ear. She squealed with delight at whatever he told her and came running towards her.

Sophie smiled as Andy met her gaze. He looked smart in blue jeans minus the usual paint smears and a blue short sleeve shirt. Sophie flashed him a bright smile and fiddled unconsciously with her finger nails.

'Miss Harris, Miss Harris, Miss Harris!'

'Yes Annabel sweetheart, what is it?' she jolted back into the present and crouched down to meet the little girl's eye. 'Are you ready to show your daddy what a star you are?'

'Yes Miss, he said to give you this Miss,' she held out her sweaty palm to reveal a crushed daisy.

'Ah, thank you sweetheart,' she smiled, taking the daisy and dropping it into a shallow glass of water nearby. 'Thank you. Now, can you lead the others onto the stage?' Annabel took the command easily as the other children who had now gathered followed her lead up the steps and took their places in front of the badly assembled choir.

'Good luck,' Linda whispered coming to join Sophie at the side of the stage. Jimmy's voice was the loudest, not a word out of place so far.

'So you really thought I meant Edward Taylor?' Sophie whispered into Linda's ear. Linda gave her a look of despair.

'I'm sorry, all you said was Taylor and I just assumed.'

Sophie giggled at her. 'How could you think I'd fancy that old twit?' Linda laughed and clapped a hand over her mouth. The children carried on as the two women stifled giggles, until Linda grabbed Sophie's arm hard. She flinched.

'What's up?' she smiled, 'wet your knickers giggling?' she smirked.

'Sort of,' Linda whispered, her face a picture of terror. Sophie looked down to a puddle on the floor. 'I think my water just broke,' Linda whispered. 'Oh my God!'

'Ssh…ssh,' Sophie hissed. 'Come with me,' she led Linda out the fire escape at the back of the hall. 'I'll take you to the hospital. Can you hold on here? My car is all the way over there. I'll have to drive over the grass. Stay here,' she commanded leaving Linda gripping onto a handrail, her knuckles white with the tension. 'Don't you dare move. I mean it,' Sophie wagged a finger at her as she ran away.

'Soph!' Linda called.

'I'll be right back,' she sprinted to the car, clutching her handbag frantically.

Sophie jerked the car roughly over the green, tyre tracks spreading along the neat lawn. The head was not going to be pleased but it was too bad. She flew out the car and opened the passenger door, helped Linda in and tossed her a towel from her gym bag that normally resided in the boot.

'Right, let's go,' she cried. Linda was moaning, clutching her stomach. 'Are you ok?'

'I'll be fine, just drive, don't panic' Linda said in-between moans. 'I need to breath slowly,' she was panting now, heavily. Sophie tried hard to concentrate on the road. The hospital was all the way over in Ipswich, a good fifteen miles.

'It's ok,' Linda was saying, 'it won't be that quick,' she attempted a sideways smile at Sophie.

'You're sure?' Sophie didn't look convinced. 'Here,' she said, tossing her mobile to Linda. 'Call Paul; just in case. At the very least he can meet us there.'

The traffic was predictably bad and at one point Sophie jumped a red light. A silver of grey filtered across the afternoon sky as they raced towards the Ipswich ring road.

'So, look, Andy is single, right?' Sophie asked, darting a glance from the blurry vision of the road for a split second. Linda had her eyes squeezed closed, her face contorted in pain, the colour of burnt amber. She sighed and moaned, her panting growing more urgent. 'Sorry,' Sophie offered. Dust flew up like a cloud around the closed windows of the car as they dashed along the single track lane. Sophie prayed no one was coming in the other direction.

'Do we...do we have...to...talk about...this...now?' Linda managed in-between breaths. Sophie gave her a half smile. Leaves cascaded up into spirals as they sped further down the country lane. A few minutes and they would reach the ring road.

'I'm sorry,' Sophie called over the roaring engine. The clouds were thickening in the sky like sodden blobs of cotton wool.

'Yes!' Linda screamed. 'As far...as...I know!' She screwed clumps of her skirt into her fist and gritted her teeth.

'We're almost at the ring road,' Sophie told her, 'have you tried Paul or do you want me to?'

Linda gave her a stunned look and concentrated hard on dialling her husband's number.

'You're mad,' Linda cried, putting Sophie's mobile to her ear. 'You can't...ring...you'll kill...us,' another deep throated moan. 'Slow down,' she yelled. 'It'll be...ages....ages...yet. Paul! It's started...yes...Soph is taking...me...ok,' she said into the phone. 'See you there,' she snapped the phone shut. As Sophie cornered the car around the last bend the mobile fell with a thud to the passenger foot-well. The ring road was in sight.

'Ok, we can slow down now,' Sophie said, realising she had been holding her breath. 'I just didn't want you to be stuck on that lane,' she explained. 'At least now we're in easy access for an ambulance,' she gasped, her breath coming back in spasms. 'Ok, how are you doing?' she chanced a look as she changed lanes towards the hospital.

'Fine,' Linda smiled, 'they're about seven minutes apart'

'What? The contractions?' a look of fear washed over Sophie's face and Linda managed a faint giggle. A patter of rain drops smattered the windscreen. That was all they needed, people slowing down.

'You said you had ages, that's not long at all!' she yelped frantically, her foot hitting down on the accelerator again.

'No, no, it's ok,' Linda breathed deeply, thrust back into her seat with the sudden quickening of the car. 'It'll be a little while...Paul...is going...to meet...us...there,' she finished, her skirt now crinkled into balls where she had been clutching at it. 'He's right...near the...hospital...already.'

'We're almost there,' Sophie said more to herself than to Linda. The headmaster was going to be so mad, she thought. 'We're almost there,' she repeated taking in a deeper breath and slowing for the traffic lights on the interchange.

'Don't worry,' Linda soothed, patting Sophie's arm as they stopped in the queue of traffic. 'You're doing a great job,' she said. Sophie cast her a smile.

'I'm supposed to be telling you that!' she laughed.

'Go for it,' Linda told her 'with Andy,' she beamed. 'He looks nice and I'm sure he's single.'

'Thanks,' Sophie smiled at her friend, a moment of calm amongst the manic afternoon. 'I'll call him later,' she said. Linda patted her arm again and then returned her fists to her suffering skirt and let out a high-pitched scream.

'What's up?' Sophie shrieked, the panic settling over her body like a fine mist.

'An...another...con...contract...ion' Linda screwed up her face.

'Come on lights!' Sophie yelled as they turned to amber. 'Get a move on!' she shouted at the car in front. 'Hold on Linda, hold on,' she called as they switched lanes and dashed up the final road. 'We're nearly there, I promise.'

'Ok' Linda gasped. 'It's ok...look!' Sophie spotted Paul's car screaming into the hospital car park just as they entered from the other direction. He flew open the door and sprinted across the car park towards them.

Sophie pulled up the handbrake as Paul opened Linda's door and was already helping her out the car. He tossed his car keys at Sophie.

'Here,' he called 'can you park it?' Sophie nodded at them both with a big grin.

'Thank you,' Linda called after her as they neared the entrance. Sophie gave them a wave. A nurse approached them with a wheelchair. Sophie watched them go into the hospital, the miracle of life about to begin.

Sophie parked up properly, proceeded to park Paul's car and slotted enough money into the ticket machine to keep him going for four hours. Hopping into the hospital she bought a bouquet of white carnations and headed for the maternity unit.

A prim nurse with brown hair stepped forward, took the keys and flowers and promised to call her with any news. Sophie thanked her and returned to her car.

The rain was falling quite heavily as she drove back to the school. The fete would be over by now she thought. The journey back to Atwood was extraordinarily slow. The school loomed up in her field of vision. Very few cars were left, the odd straggling parent eating up the remains of iced digestives. The hall was virtually empty when she returned. The headmaster stood in the middle of the hall looking distinctly lost.

'Ah, Sophie my dear, wherever did you get to? I tried to obtain a round of applause for your efforts with the play but you were nowhere to be found!' he looked at her quizzically, his fingers gripping the edges of his tank top protectively.

'I'm sorry, Linda went into labour,' she puffed. 'I had to take her to the hospital. I'm sorry, I've only just got back.'

The headmaster's hands went to his mouth, forming a perfect O.

'Goodness gracious, is she doing ok?' he looked around the hall. 'Thank goodness she didn't have the baby here!' he attempted a laugh, a strained expression of relief.

'Quite,' Sophie agreed, amused by his reaction.

'I thought her due date was three weeks away?' he looked genuinely confused.

'Babies do come early,' Sophie told him earnestly. 'They'll arrive when they want to, which is rarely convenient,' she said, suppressing a grin.

'I suppose so, yes,' the headmaster nodded gravely. 'Oh dear. Well, well. You will keep me abreast of any news won't you Sophie my dear?'

'Yes Sir, of course,' she smiled. 'Is everything sorted here or do you need me to stay?' she gestured around the hall, devoid of all but the cleaners, who had been drafted in at great expense according to the headmaster.

'No, no, we're done here I think. You'll take the stage back for me dear, won't you?' he began to walk away, 'next week will do,' he said as an afterthought. 'You get yourself off home now my dear,' he called.

Great, she said to herself. Bloody marvellous, still, it gave her a valid reason for phoning Andy...

It had been an eventful day. Sophie parked in the driveway and opened the front door. Cautiously she looked at the doormat but it was clear. She heaved a sigh of relief and kicked off her shoes. It was almost six o'clock when she curled into the settee and picked up the corded phone by the window, her fingers trembling slightly as she dialled Andy's number that she now knew by heart.

'Hello.' She smiled at the sound of his voice.

'You'll never guess,' she whispered into the receiver. 'I've got to take the stage back to the community hall.'

The rain had died and the evening sunset was glorious, the red crisp lines cutting through the skyline savagely. Sophie watched the clouds, now lighter than earlier, drifting in the light breeze. Dusk was settling around the town, filtering down like a blanket.

'Ah no, and you want me to help you I suppose?' his voice was warm like treacle. Sophie felt her skin tingling as she curled up her toes on the settee.

'I could do it by myself but I thought a professional would do a much better job!' she teased, twirling the lounge phone cord between her fingers absent-mindedly. The lounge felt warmer since the painting had been completed. Everything was warmer suddenly.

'Yeah right, like you're going to lift and stack those wooden crates in your tiny car! When did you have in mind?' he sighed jokingly. She could hear his smile down the phone line as she twiddled affectionately with the cord.

'Thank you,' she giggled. 'How about tomorrow? If it's out the way before Monday it'll give me bonus points with the headmaster, not that I should need any. I've got to take on Linda's classes next week too.'

'I searched for you today,' he said a mild hint of accusation lurking in the recess of his voice. 'Where'd you get to?'

'Didn't you hear? Linda went into labour, right about the time the play started. I had to take her to Ipswich General.'

'Oh' he said shortly. 'How is she?'

'Ok, I haven't heard yet. Paul, her husband, sent me a text to say she and the baby were ok. A little boy, seven pounds five, apparently. By the time I got back everyone had gone. How did the play go? I bet your Annabel blew them away. She's a little star.'

'Great,' Andy exclaimed. 'She was brilliant. I'll get her to tell you about it on Monday, not that she wouldn't have anyway. You do know that she'll want to do another play before long?' his voice taking on a sound of warning.

'Will she? I suppose so, well,' Sophie smiled, 'we'll have to see what we can fix up for her won't we,' she said. 'I am in charge of English and literacy,' she boasted. 'I'm sure we can sort something out.'

'I'm sure we can,' he agreed. 'We make a good team you and I.'

'You know my friend, Linda, she confused you with someone else,' Sophie blurted out, her reactions ten paces ahead of her brain.

'What'd you mean?' his voice clipped.

'I told her about you when I first hired you for the DIY and she thought...' Sophie paused, was it wise to tell him this?

'What did she think?' he wanted to know. 'I've always wondered what women find to talk about,' the sound of his laughter putting her at ease.

'She thought you were Mr Edward Taylor,' Sophie said.

'Who?'

'There's another Annabel in the school with the surname Taylor...'

'Ah, well my little Annabel, much as I'd love her to have my name, is Weston. I fought over it long and hard with her mother when she was engaged to Tony and she said it was easier for Annabel if they all had the same name. Sometimes I wish I'd fought harder, but I suppose I can see her point.'

'Um, sorry,' Sophie said. 'It must be hard for you.'

'Not really,' he mused. 'Most of the time she's home with her mother and Tony. She only stays with me the odd weekend night. I've had to stay there before to take her to school the next morning, when they've gone away for their naughty little breaks, but truth be told, I'd much rather she come to mine. It's easier for me. Why'd it matter anyway, who Linda thought I was?'

'It doesn't, I mean it doesn't now,' Sophie spluttered. 'Anyway, Linda thought you were him so she said you were married...because...'

'...because Edward Taylor is married,' Andy finished. 'Well, I'm not, I'm very,' his voice softened, a sultry tone '...very single. Actually no,' he stopped. Sophie felt her breath catch in her throat. 'I am but hopefully not for much longer. There's someone I want to ask out.'

'Oh,' Sophie said, 'well I'd better go...'

'No, Soph, wait, you've got the wrong end of the stick,' the words tumbled from his mouth in a rush. 'It's you. I want to ask you out. Do you fancy going for a drink sometime?'

'Yes,' Sophie blurted. 'Absolutely. I mean, yes, I'd like that. I'm sorry I thought you meant...'

'Yeah, I know, I didn't phrase it very well. Sorry. Remind me not to do subtly, I'm obviously crap at it!' he laughed.

'Oh,' she laughed. Suddenly her laugher died. If he was single who was he buying a cuddling bear and roses for? 'Um, what about the roses?' she blurted out, throwing her hand over her mouth the second the words were out. 'Sorry, I meant, it's just...it's just that I saw you in Tesco's and you were buying roses and giant teddy bear,' she protested.

'Oh that,' he laughed. 'That was nothing. I thought Annabel would like the bear and the roses well...' he took a deep breath. 'They were for my mother,' he finished. 'It was her birthday and I wanted to put them on her grave.'

'Oh my god, I'm so sorry. I'm sorry, I didn't mean to...'

'Hey, Soph, it's all right. It's been years. Honestly,' he began to chuckle. 'You must have really been confused.'

'Yeah, well,' she found her voice again. 'I was. It's nice to know I'm not going crazy,' she replied.

'So what about that drink then?' he tried again, 'what do you say?'

'In that case you'd better come and pick me up!' she challenged. 'I can teach you about subtly,' she smiled.

'Yes Miss,' he teased.

Chapter Fourteen

April 1936

Katie sat at her writing desk, her hand shaking badly. She took a deep breath and looked at the blank sheet of paper before her. Where to begin? How did you write a confession? They hadn't taught her that at finishing school. She had sent Albert out on the golf course with his friends. She did not have long and she knew she had to get it done before he came home. She still hadn't told him about the horrible day, even after they had watched Frederick bury the bodies in the garden.

'It is better that you don't know,' she had said.

The guilt of keeping the secret from him was almost too much to bear. That was why, not only why, but another valid reason for her to write her confession. She had never kept a secret from her husband since their wedding day. She believed that was the key to the success of their marriage and keeping her knowledge of that fateful day from him was slowly killing her. She had to get it out of her, onto the white page in front of her. Perhaps then it would stop eating her alive.

With another deep breath she closed her eyes and forced herself to think carefully about every detail. It would be important it was accurate, just in case it was ever found. She knew exactly what she was going to do with the confession and she didn't know if there would be any repercussions, but she had decided she would have to live with the risk. It was better than living with the certain knowledge that she may be the only witness to the crime.

After what felt like an eternity Katie folded the confession in half and half again. She slid it into an envelope and wrote briefly on the front. Confession & Statement of Mrs Katie Bass, April 1936. *Then she left a note on the hall telephone table telling Albert she was going next door to see Frederick.*

'Hello Fred,' Katie said, 'I wanted to see how you were doing today?' Frederick opened the door himself, wider to let Katie in. 'I've bought you a casserole' she said, proffering the ceramic bowl in her hands. 'I had cook make an extra one for you. Just heat it in the oven for twenty minutes to warm it up' she said, leading the way to the kitchen and placing it on the work surface by the cooker. 'Where is Betsy?'

'I dismissed her, all of them,' Frederick said quietly. 'I don't want them here.'

'Oh Fred, I understand. If there's anything we can do to help you have only to ask. One understands how difficult it must be, truly.'

'Thank you,' Frederick said. His eyes were quite red and his locally famous temper had diminished into a vapour. 'Elise is,' he gulped a lungful of air. 'Still...in Cornwall' he stammered, 'seems her grandmother...her grandmother is quite ill and...and, she may be gone for some time,' he struggled through the sentence.

Katie gave him a quizzical look. So that was the story he was going to weave then.

'I've also bought you this.' Katie left the note on the work surface next to the casserole. 'I know what happened to them but don't worry I won't breath a word,' she said. 'You can read it if you want. You can destroy it if you want to, I don't care, but I had to have my say. Please, don't tell me what you do with it. I don't want to know. I need to think I have told the truth.' Frederick looked at her stunned.

'But...how?'

'I don't want to talk about it Frederick,' Katie touched his arm softly and he leant into her and cried on her shoulder. Katie comforted him as best she could, led him towards the kitchen table and encouraged him to sit down. It was pitiful to see a grown man cry but in her heart she knew he felt guilty for the wasted years. It was all such a terrible waste she reflected. Such a lovely woman…

'Does Bert…?' Frederick looked up from his hands and Katie shook her head.

'No, no I didn't tell him. I don't want him to suffer the torment. There are enough people already affected. I don't need to say another thing on the matter, I swear, unless of course you need someone to talk to,' she smiled at him fleetingly. 'Try to remember the good times,' she soothed. 'That's what I'm doing.' Frederick nodded at her in silence and then, as if the thought had only just occurred to him.

'Will you help me plant some roses?' he asked, 'out there by the conifers? To remember…'

Katie smiled at him and nodded.

'Yes of course I will, let's do it now,' she whispered.

Katie and Frederick had dug deep into the soft earth in front of the baby trees at the rear perimeter of the garden. Katie dropped the tiny rose bushes into the holes and Frederick covered them with the moist soil. It had taken a while and she was not used to manual labour so Frederick had taken most of the effort on himself. They worked in silence, each shedding the odd tear. When the last bulb was in place Frederick picked up the watering can and sprinkled the water copiously along the flowerbed. Then, in quiet reflection he prayed, fell to his knees and cried softly.

A depressive chill over-shadowed the dusk-lit room. The winter air whistled in through the open windows in the conservatory. Frederick has begun not to notice things like temperature. His doctor has told him he needs to take better care of himself but he fails to do so, thinking all the time that there is little point in continuing in his existence he dares to call a life.

He has appointed a local woman "to do" for him three times a week and a cook who visits daily, but further than that he does not keep company. He does not even attend Coates any more. His mother sits in her sitting room criticising Elise's sudden disappearance with the utmost distaste.

Elise has gone and he misses the way she organised his life for him, laid out his clothes, oversaw the household, the laundry, picked up his clothes from the floor where he carelessly discarded them each night. She stitched his socks and starched his collars, despite the staff being more than capable of doing so directly. She kept the house he called his and not theirs, and tolerated his forbearing mother day after day. She never answered back, never argued with him or Clarissa, never gave him any grief, any stress, anything negative. She nursed him when he was unwell, cared for his possessions and was always there for him.

She did everything and he never once said thank you.

Frederick could hear Clarissa chastising the cook and wondered what would become of him now that Elise had gone. Clarissa of course thought Elise would return "from Cornwall" when her fictitious grandmother had regained her health. A great mistake that had been; he had forgotten in his haste that Elise had no family.

'I don't look forward to her return Frederick,' Clarissa had warned. 'A woman does not abandon her husband, whatever her excuse may be. I shall find out where she has really gone and see to it that she is fully aware of her failings. You needn't worry yourself on that score my boy, I shall talk to her for you!'

Now, he sits at his old oak desk, regretting every possible second when he could have treated her better, acknowledged her presence in the very least. He regrets it all because her death was his fault. He took her to the edge day after day and finally she slipped into the darkness. All of it he lays at his own hand. It was time to confess his sins.

Methodically, as is his way, Frederick takes out a leaf of cream writing paper and a fountain pen. He begins to write, pausing to think of the exact phrase to convey his suffering and his own remorse.

After a minute he looks up, looks around himself as if seeing it for the first time. His house is neatly furnished, not richly for he had never lavished money on her housekeeping desires, but for the first time he notices that it displays a greater wealth than it actually possesses. It's an art, he decides, one, which his late wife had been very good at. He notices the dust now beginning to show on the mantle piece because he hasn't the inclination, nor the sufficient staff to pick up the duster. He notices the floor, the breadcrumbs beginning to gather and the papers forming their own mountain by the doormat. She really didn't deserve her fate. He continues to write, determined to set the record straight.

Every day he wakes, attempts to feel better, fails and then spends hours feeling guilty about being so miserable when all around him there is news of people dying of starvation. He lines up in the ration queue, takes his measly allowance and feels awful when he hasn't even touched it before the perishables have to be thrown out. He tells himself he would be better off joining the forces, and he would do, if they would have him but he is too old now. It really is too late for everything.

The candle he has lit is burning slowly as the darkness descends into the room, the curtains drawn. An eternity seemed to have passed but Frederick hadn't noticed, his pen working furiously until he felt spent and tired.

When he is finished he rests the pen on the blotter and carefully folds the paper, placing it into a co-ordinating envelope, sealing it in a style he thinks she would have approved of. He kisses the seal and rises from his chair.

The hallway is now very dark, the dusky evening having transformed into night. He flicks on the electric lamp and the hallway is certainly very clear. Everything is now very clear to him. He has been blind, he thinks to himself, too blind for far too long. Now that it is too late he can see what he should have done, how he should have behaved, how he should have... It is all ifs and buts now. Academic as it makes precious little difference now.

Resolutely he opens his hand-crafted wooden box. He places the envelope into the depths of the unseen, amidst the marriage certificate, letters he once wrote to Elise and she to him in their courting days. On top of his own letter he rests the statement from Katie and slowly mounts the stairs to the landing. At the top of the stairs near the bathroom door is the attic loft hatch. Frederick carries a dining chair to the base of the hatch and stands on it gingerly. He lifts the edge of the hatch. It creates a gap, just wide enough for him to slide the box into the loft. Then, he goes to bed, cries bitterly into his hands, closes his eyes and hopes not to open them again.

Several weeks pass uneventfully before Clarissa suffers a fatal heart attack and Frederick finds himself truly alone for the first time. He misses Elise more than ever.

Chapter Fifteen

May 2009

The Hoover was making an uncertain noise as Sophie shoved it around the landing. The painting was all but completed. Even the stairway, previously dark, was now bursting with light. She eyed it all happily. Biased she may be, but Andy really was a genius. Record time too. The Hoover suddenly gnawed on a chunk of newspaper that lay on the carpet; a forgotten link in the stretching of the dust sheet over the landing. It crunched is way up the pipe and ground to a halt in protest.

'Great,' Sophie tutted at it and began to pull it apart. She held the long pipe nozzle above her head, gripping with both hands to divorce it from the suction end. 'What, is it glued on?' she cried. With a heave it came free, the suction end smashing into the attic hatch, lifting and sliding it clean away so a nasty black hole gaped down at her. 'Great,' she spluttered again, selecting her dressing table chair from the bedroom and balancing precariously to put the hatch door back in place.

A shaft of light from the landing window cast a rectangular silhouette. Sophie dug her face into the depths of the empty attic and looked around. A small hand crafted wooden box was there, within easy reach of the loft door. She dragged it towards her, ate a cloud of thick dust and coughed. Gradually she bought it closer to her and climbed down with the box. The dust littered the landing next to the jammed up Hoover.

Intrigued she took it to her bedroom and sat at the dressing table. The key cried out in agony as she turned it in the small lock of the box. The lock itself had rusted harshly over the

174

years so that it was almost stuck but the creaky key twisted slowly and eventually a tiny click told her that the secrets had been released once more.

She leafed anxiously through the various letters and photographs, faded wispy sheets that gave away their age by the tea colour stained folds and the ink letters that leapt from the page with emotion and anticipation. They had been gathered in bundles, saved in date order and tied in red ribbon. 'Just exactly as they should be kept' she said aloud to herself, with approval, a nice wooden box, never to be thrown, yet stored away in the depths of the memory bank. Beneath all the letters, photographs, marriage and death certificates were two letters in an unknown hand. She unfolded the first one and held her breath at the first line.

To Whom It May Concern:

I killed Thomas Brody. It was a mistake. It all happened last November. I heard the noise from next door. Albert was out, nowhere to be seen. It was about three in the afternoon and I heard some screams. I knew it was Elise Harris screaming so I ran next door. When I got there she was dead, Cheryl Brody had stabbed her in the chest. Thomas Brody was still alive, he was in a panic, crying, shouting at Cheryl, and running around the room not knowing what to do. After a second they both saw me and that was it. I saw Cheryl holding the knife, covered in blood. Elise's blood.

I panicked, I wanted to run away, but it was too late. Cheryl was behind me; shoved me into the room and closed the front door. She asked if I had called anyone but I hadn't so I said no. She shoved me toward the corner of the room and I screamed; she came towards me with the knife still in her hand. I screamed and she shoved her hand over my mouth. It was horrible, all bloody and warm.

Thomas was still running around at a loose end. I gathered she wasn't going to kill him, she wanted him alive, to stay with her instead of eloping with Elise.

She reached up with the knife, coming down quickly and I thought I was going to die but suddenly Thomas had come out

175

of his trance. He wrestled it from her, for a long time the three of us fought over custody of the lethal weapon. Thomas and I were trying to get the knife from her. She was strong, she held onto it tightly and then in a moment when I don't quite know what happened Thomas moved behind her and between us we had hold of her arm but she yanked free and all I saw was his face, the pain across his eyes. She had stabbed him, she hadn't wanted too, she fell beside him on the floor but it was already too late for Thomas. He was dead.

Then she spun on me, accused me, said it was my fault he was dead. I thought that was it but she held the knife to my throat and said she had another use for me. In a few months she would go to the police, she said, and say she knew who had killed Elise and Thomas. She was going to frame me for it. I was scared, when she let me go I ran. I ran home as fast as I could and I sat in the bathroom and cried for hours.

I'm not sure what happened exactly, but I think I may have killed Thomas Brody. For that I'm truly sorry, it wasn't intentional.

Mrs Katie Bass
Neighbour to Elise & Frederick Harris
April 1936

So much for the police, Sophie thought, who needed them now. She supposed she would have to take the box to the police station. Just as she was gathering strength to stand up she noticed a second letter and took it up, wondering if she could withstand any more surprises.

As God is my witness I must tell someone about this horrible business. I must confess my sins. I was bound to be a suspect, a good one at that when you think about all those horrible rows we had. The neighbours, the Basses, they must have heard us.

I didn't kill Elise. She was having an affair with Mr Thomas Brody, and they were going to elope, to run away together. It was my stupid pride that cut me off from almost everyone else, and most importantly from Elise. And I'm sorry about that; I'm sorry, really sorry.

I subjected her to a life of drudgery and worst still, to my mother, who love her as I did was a tyrant of a woman. She ruled everything and everyone within the reach of her influence and I am afraid that I fell under that spell and did nothing to protect my wife from it either.

I've been so stupid over the years. Too proud and too stupid to give in when I should have just done what most people would have done. I found them, together, dead on the living room floor. It was awful, all their blood everywhere. They had been stabbed, both in the chest. She wouldn't have suffered I don't think, that was some small comfort. You see I couldn't bear to lose her, that's why I buried her in the garden. At least in death she would have been with me. I'm hoping we will be together again in a few days. I don't have much longer; funny but I do know that somehow. They say you know when your time is up and that's true, my time is nearly up now.

I think Mrs Brody killed them both. That was Thomas's wife. I never met her but I overheard them talking one day, Elise and Tom. I heard him telling her that Cheryl was really jealous, was making life difficult for him to leave, wouldn't just accept that he didn't want her anymore. To some extent I could understand but then I always knew she was never really in love with me. It was always just something better than before for my Elise. Something more stable, more permanent. I tried my best to be the man she would have wanted but in the end I couldn't be anything else. Tom was what she wanted and I wasn't going to stand in her way any longer. Not after all the hell I had given her about such stupid things in the past.

You mellow with age you know. I'm hoping this note will find its way to the police one day. They can use it to catch Cheryl if she is still around. I'm convinced it was her who killed them but of course I wasn't here at the time. I was at my club. Mother would have been out to coffee that afternoon; it was her usual day. I'm not sure what happened to the staff, they would normally have been present but I suspect Elise sent

177

them out. She was a bright woman, such intelligence that sadly I failed to appreciate until it was all too late.

I'm sorry I didn't tell anyone but I was convinced they would have arrested me for the charge of murder and in jail I wouldn't have had Elise nearby.

Oddly enough Mother died shortly after that horrible day. Who knows, perhaps we could have had a proper life together after all. Elise could have taken her rightful place as lady of the house. Maybe she would finally have been happy and maybe I would have had a second chance at keeping her.

Life is full of ifs and buts. All that matters in the end is to be happy. I wish I had learnt that lesson sooner.
Frederick Harris
April 1936

Sophie gathered up the box quickly and turned the rusty key until the contents were safely locked away. She dusted herself down hurriedly and leapt over the vacuum cleaner. She had to take the box to the police; it was the news they were all waiting for. It was unlikely but if Cheryl was still alive maybe she was the poison pen…

'Can you meet me at the police station?' she shouted, her mobile swirling around the lap of her skirt as she drove hastily towards the police station. Sophie squinted in the low sun at the road ahead of her.

'Sure, sure, calm down, what's happened?' Andy asked, 'I can't hear you properly,' he said, pressing the phone even tighter against his red ear.

'I'm sorry' she called, 'it's my phone. I'm driving. I've put it on loudspeaker, haven't got hands-free,' she explained. 'Can you meet me? I really…' her voice collapsed '…need you,' she finished lamely.

'Sure, are you ok?' Andy could hear the breeze from her open car window whistling down the line like crackle.

'Yeah, I just really need you,' she cried. 'I'll explain everything when you get there,' she called into her lap, taking a twist into a left turn and slowing for the roundabout. In the traffic line she picked up the phone. 'Thank you,' she said, 'I've got to go now, I'm moving again,' she flicked it closed and tossed it over to the empty passenger seat as she cruised the little car towards the roundabout and indicated right into the road where Atwood police station had resided for the past hundred years.

She sat in the chilly waiting foyer clutching the wooden box tightly; the desk Sergeant eyeing her in between phone calls. Inspector Allen would be with her in five minutes she was assured. Five minutes passed and again she was assured the inspector was on his way along the dingy corridors as they spoke.

The surplus dust from the attic decorated the blouse she had knotted over a white cami top and jeans. It was housework day and she was aware she didn't look exactly glamorous but the desk sergeant's eyes kept straying her way.

'He is on his way Miss, I promise,' he said leaning heavily out over the counter. He picked up the ringing phone again as Andy bounced through the doors. Sophie leapt up and crashed into him, the wooden box smashing into his chest.

'I found this,' she thrust the box at him. 'I'm sorry,' her eyes pleaded with him. 'I really needed...'

'Hey, that's ok,' he stroked some dust from her hair. 'What is it?'

'Statements,' she exclaimed, 'from 1935,' she nodded her head.

'What?'

'Miss Harris?' Sergeant Wells was at the door. 'This way please.'

'Come on,' she whispered to Andy. They followed Wells towards Inspector's Allen's smoke-filled office. As Wells opened the door the desk drawer slammed shut. A tell-tale swirl of white mist seeped guiltily from the desk. Sophie cast a sly smile. He really wasn't very good at breaking the law, just as well he was on the enforcement side, he'd never had made a successful villain.

'Miss Harris,' he indicated a chair 'nice to see you again.' Sophie noticed his brown checked hat on the stand by the door. The inspector looked at Andy. 'And…?'

'Andrew Taylor,' he extended his hand then sat in the chair next to Sophie.

'What can I do for you?' Inspector Allen addressed Sophie as he lowered his tall frame back into his wheeled chair, the squeak as he sat increasing to a crescendo. 'I haven't had any further leads if that's what you're here for…'

'Yes you have,' Sophie challenged 'as of now.' The box dropped the last inch from her grasp with a thud on the inspector's desk. 'Open it,' she offered. 'The key is a bit rusty but it does work.' The inspector eyed her cautiously and looked at Wells who was perched on his desk like a bird of prey. Inspector Allen tweaked his moustache thoughtfully and nodded his head at Wells who bounced forward as if on a spring. The key squeaked in protest as he spun it slowly. 'I found this in the attic today,' Sophie explained. 'It has statements and letters inside from 1935, and the marriage certificate belonging to Frederick and Elise Harris.' Inspector Allen, Sergeant Wells and Andy all stared at her sceptically. 'Yes, that's right,' she affirmed. 'See for yourself. There is a witness statement of the murders and a confession of burial from Frederick.'

Sergeant Wells selected a pair of tweezers from his pocket and leafed out the ribbon bound letters, one bunch at a time until they lay in a row in front of the inspector.

'I've touched them myself,' Sophie said, 'but that's it. Looks like it's been undisturbed since the day it was put in the attic.'

'Would you care for some coffee?' the inspector asked, pressing a buzzer on his internal phone without waiting for their answers.

'Um, yes, thank you,' Sophie agreed. 'Both white, no sugar,' she told him. The inspector repeated her order into the phone and returned to the box before him.

'Surely Miss someone would have accessed the attic since it being put in there and your inheriting the house some seventy years later!' he cried, his gaze temporarily diverted from the statement that Wells was now laying out in front of him.

'No, not necessarily,' Sophie said. 'They didn't have many possessions in the thirties Inspector. Times were hard. The house passed from Frederick to his brother Rodney. Frederick was 76 when he died and Rodney was already 69 when he inherited. Chances are he didn't have much use for the attic.'

Sophie watched the inspector flatten out the statements from Frederick and their neighbour, Katie Bass.

'The house then went to my grandmother,' she continued. 'She was already fifty when she inherited. You see I'm the first relatively young person to move into the house since Frederick died. No-one has had any need to go in the attic. It hasn't been sold so no surveyor has been round. It's just passed from person to person, untouched as it were. Even I haven't used the loft so far, since I came from a tiny little place.'

'Where did you come from?' Wells enquired, his gaze still on the ribbon bound letters that were now poured out over Inspector Allen's desk like a collage.

'Excuse me?'

'Where did you live before Miss?'

'Sutton Street,' she said shortly. 'It was a little place, no room for clutter,' she said, tilting her head slightly. 'The house is far too big for me really, I've nowhere near enough things to fill it,' she smiled. 'Not yet, anyway.'

A female police constable knocked the door open with a tray of mugs and rested it heavily on the edge of the inspector's desk.

'Thank you Hazel,' he smiled at her as she handed the mugs out. When Hazel had gone the inspector took a large gulp of his super-strong tea.

'Ah, I needed that,' he sighed. 'Thank you Miss Harris,' Inspector Allen spoke firmly. 'Thank you for bringing this in for us. We'll have to hang onto it for a while I'm afraid.'

'Oh yes, I know,' Sophie said smiling at Andy who sat silently next to her, his face a picture of disbelief. 'Can I have it back though? When you're finished?'

'I can let you have the box but I can't promise you these letters,' he cast her a sly smile. 'Not all of them anyway, some may be relevant to the case you see and they'll be kept as evidence, especially these,' he nodded at the statements. 'But the box is yours, soon as we've dusted it for prints. Oh yes,' he poked a bony finger up in the air. 'That reminds me, you say you've handled this yourself Miss?' Sophie nodded at him, taking a sip of the hot coffee. 'We probably won't get any other sets from the box after all this time anyway,' the inspector smiled. 'I'll let you know Miss' he nodded at Wells who leapt up to open the door. Sophie and Andy took the hint, rising from their seats in unison, their virtually untouched coffee mugs steaming on the desk.

'Thank you Inspector,' Sophie said, her hair bouncing as they turned towards the door to leave. 'Oh, Inspector…'

'Yes?'

'It's probably not relevant but I think my grandmother may have suspected something.'

'What makes you think that?' Inspector Allen chewed on the end of his pencil.

'Just something my dad said, anyway, her prints may be on the box I guess…'

'Ok, thank you.' Inspector Allen nodded curtly and returned to some paperwork on his desk. Sophie and Andy left.

As Wells closed the door the inspector indicated Sophie's coffee cup with a quick nod, the sunlight bouncing off his greyish hair in the dart-like movement.

'Take her prints,' he said to Wells, 'from her coffee mug so we can eliminate hers from the box. Don't suppose we'll get any others but if we do they could be the grandmothers. Let me know if there are more than three sets because the third set could be the killers.'

Wells stretched a latex glove over his hand. It snapped down on his wrist. He picked up Sophie's abandoned mug, tipped the dregs into a nearby plant pot, the grateful occupant sucking it up as if it were Christmas, and slid the mug into a large plastic evidence bag.

'I'm off to forensics then Sir,' Wells reported 'I'll let you know soon as they've got the report.'

At Well's exit Inspector Allen opened his desk drawer. A cloud of smoke commanded the air in front of him. He inhaled deeply and smiled. A brief knock at the door startled him and he bolted the drawer closed as the desk sergeant breezed in with a fistful of messages. He would have to be more careful, he thought, one day he would get caught in the act.

Sophie and Andy sat happily in the familiar corner seats. Andy smiled and watched her take the glass of wine to her lips. The pub was quieter this time in the absence of the live band. Instead the pub's sound system was playing its own easy listening music that seemed to blend into the walls and filter around the air like an atmospheric cloud.

'I hear the play went well,' Sophie remarked, 'sorry I missed most of it.'

'Yeah, pity since you put so much work into it,' he replied. 'You know, Annabel really likes you. She said you were her favourite teacher,' he confessed with a wide grin and took a sip from his pint of bitter.

'That's probably because she likes English and she's good at reading,' Sophie reasoned. 'Kids don't tend to like anything, including the teacher, about the subjects they find more difficult.'

'No, no,' he disagreed, shaking his head in defiance, 'she genuinely likes you.'

'Really?' Sophie quizzed, her head tilted to the right. She took another sip of wine and rested the glass down on the cardboard coaster.

'Really,' he affirmed

'I hardly teach Annabel as it happens. Although I guess I will be now, since I've got to take over Linda's classes too. Still, she doesn't know me that well.'

'Yet,' Andy smiled. Sophie eyed him slyly.

'Well, good,' she stammered slightly, 'it's good she likes me. You can tell her I like her too.'

'Yep, it sure is,' Andy declared, 'and I will.' They sat motionless, leaning in over the table. Sophie felt a rush of heat rising up her body, Andy's eyes delving into the very depths of her soul.

Crash, the sound of breaking glass and Sophie was thrown out of the dreamlike subconscious world. They twisted their heads to watch the barman disappear beneath the counter and bob up and down, each time producing further fragments of shattered glass.

'Can I ask you a question?' she looked shyly at him. 'You don't have to answer,' she assured him. 'If you don't want to talk about it.'

'You want to know what happened with Annabel's mother?' he guessed and she nodded silently. 'It's a fair question,' he agreed, took a sip of his beer and put the glass down with a quiet thud. He leant back over the table towards her as if he were going to whisper the entire story. She mirrored him, watched his lips as he spoke and looked into his eyes as he smiled at her. 'I met her when I was pretty young and stupid,' he began. 'She was a looker,' he smiled at the memory. 'Not stunning like you,' he smiled as Sophie coloured bashfully. 'But she was pretty,' he continued. 'Anyway, we went out a few times. It didn't last longer than a month. I broke it off. She was nice but she wasn't for me. She didn't take it too well' he confessed. 'Seems she wanted to get married young and start a family and I guess she thought I'd fit the bill. Anyway, I told her she'd have to find someone else for that. I didn't hear from her after that but about a month later she called me, said she had something to tell me.' He took another sip of his drink. 'Stupid really but it didn't click what she meant. Anyway, she came by my place after work one evening and then she told me, she was pregnant. I didn't believe her at first,' he admitted. 'Seemed a likely trick to get me to take her back. I know it sounds pig-headed,' he sighed.

Sophie felt her fingers travelling the surface of the table, cutting the space between them quickly and resting over his left hand. He gripped her finger with his thumb and toyed with the palm of her hand, his finger tips lightly circling.

'I insisted she take another test and I went with her to the doctors. She was right she was already six weeks pregnant. No question about it, definitely mine too. I was a bit shocked. We'd been careful, you know,' he looked at her. 'Very careful. It wasn't what I'd planned at all.'

'Things never quite turn out the way you plan do they,' Sophie whispered.

'She's fabulous though,' Andy suddenly lit up. 'Annabel I mean,' he clarified to Sophie's half laugh.

'You didn't try to patch things up with…'

'God no!' Andy exclaimed. 'I mean, I said I'd support the child and everything but there was no way I wanted a relationship with her. Harsh I know, but I had to make that quite plain. I think she was hoping for something else,' he sighed. 'Anyway, that doesn't matter now. She married that Tony when Annabel was three so it's all worked out ok.'

The music from the pub's sound system sprang into a rendition of an old beetles song. Sophie watched a group of kids hovering conspicuously by the bar. They looked too young to be served, their age given away freely as they squabbled between them for a single identification method they could doctor.

'They're never going to get served,' Andy bet, 'just look at them. 'Isn't that a school satchel on that girl's shoulder?'

'Yeah, I think it is' Sophie laughed. They watched as the barman approached them and minutes later, after much fuss, they mooched out the door with long faces. Andy chuckled and turned back in his seat.

'I'm going to see Linda and the baby tomorrow,' Sophie reported, 'do you want to come?'

'Are you sure she'll want me there, she doesn't know me,' he said.

'That's ok, she won't mind,' Sophie told him. 'I've told her all about you anyway,' she answered, 'so she almost knows you.'

'Oh I see,' he laughed, 'I'm on a back-foot before I even start! All right then, but it had better have been good things!'

'As if I'd say anything else,' she teased, taking a sip of her wine for courage and flashing him her best mock coy look.

'Shall we go after we've finished the hallway?'

'It'll be finished tomorrow?' she looked amazed. 'My, you are quick,' she teased. Andy took her hand back in his and stared into her eyes so intently that she felt her entire being froze at his command.

'Not at everything,' he whispered. Her body temperature soared, her breath dried up into a gasp and the words died on her tongue. 'It's a date,' he said, 'perhaps after that you'd like to go out for dinner?' She nodded mutely, speech momentarily eluding her. 'Good,' he said. 'I'll make a reservation,' he grinned.

The screaming pierced the skin and drilled crudely into the skull. Sophie tried not to shudder for fear of affronting Linda and Paul, whose fragile nerves were already simmering a fraction below eruption.

Paul gestured the letter T with his hands and Sophie nodded, creased her face into a polite smile and looked back at Linda.

'How many sugars?' he called over the noise.

'What?' she mouthed silently with a shrug of her shoulders.

'None,' Linda shouted above the baby's red face.

'What?' Paul was straining to hear Linda from the kitchen above the racket their baby son was producing.

'NONE!' shouted Linda hoarsely. 'I think I'm getting a sore throat,' she announced and stuck the dummy into little Alex's mouth. The silence was a blessed relief. Andy looked at Sophie, his face twisted into confusion.

'I'm not surprised,' Sophie replied, moving a pile of ironing from the settee and taking a seat. She patted the sofa and Andy obeyed, pleased to be released from the awkward standing pose.

'What's up with him?' asked Andy, fiddling with a stuffed animal 'And what is this?' he queried holding up a blue and red chequered fluffy lump.

'It's a haahoo,' Linda laughed. 'It's from the Night Garden.'

'Oh right, of course,' Andy mocked understanding. 'So, he's alright now?' nodding at the baby in slight fear.

'Oh yeah, he'll be fine now. He's been changed and fed. I had to burp him before he could have his dummy back. I'll have to teach him some patience I think,' Linda explained kissing her son lightly on the head. 'Lots of trouble aren't you little one' she smiled. Baby Alex's face was slowly returning to a normal shade.

'He has a fine set of lungs,' Andy said, accepting his tea from Paul, 'thanks.'

'Tell me about it,' Paul agreed with a sigh. 'Doesn't like sleeping much I can tell ya,' he announced as he set Sophie's tea on the table by her side. 'Do you want another one love?'

'No thanks,' Linda said rising to put Alex in his moses basket. 'Can you get me a glass of water?' Paul vanished at her request.

'I've bought you something,' Sophie told her, producing a card and a neatly wrapped blue package from her handbag. 'It's only a little thing.'

'Oh thanks hun, you didn't need to,' Linda coughed. 'Oh thanks,' she said gratefully accepting the water from Paul. 'Is it your turn or mine?'

'Yours,' Paul smiled at his wife. 'We take it in turns to open the presents,' he informed them.

The paper rustled noisily as Linda unwrapped the pale blue babygros for Alex and lavender and camomile bubble bath for her. Linda almost cried.

'Oh thank you!' she exclaimed. 'You've no idea how much I'm going to look forward to this,' she clutched the Radox bubble bath as if it were gold dust. 'Thank you hun,' she wiped a stray tear from her eye. Sophie couldn't believe it. This wasn't the strong head-first Linda she knew. It was only bubble bath.

'You're welcome,' Sophie mumbled.

'Hormones,' Paul mouthed silently from his position on the arm of Linda's chair, his arm draped over Linda's shoulders. 'Shall I put this upstairs love?' he offered. Linda reluctantly gave into Paul's grasp and he slipped quietly out the room.

'I'm glad I didn't get you two,' Sophie smiled.

The room around her was complete chaos; it looked like a hurricane had blown straight through the middle of the lounge. There were toys littering the floor, washing tossed into a basket, stacks of ironing in the most unlikely places, a new pack of nappies, baby wipes and sudocrem on a changing mat by the window, and a pile of new clothes with cards on Paul's computer desk in the far corner.

'I'm sorry, I can't seem to stop crying,' Linda smiled. 'I'm not sad, honestly. I'm fine. So, how...' Linda wiped away another tear and drank half her water quickly. '...how are you getting on with my classes?' she enquired.

'Oh, it's ok. Bit hectic though,' Sophie admitted. 'All that extra preparation, I just hope the head realises what's involved.'

'I doubt he will hun, you'll have to tell him. If they're not getting a sub in to cover me then he should be paying you extra,' Linda reasoned, 'bet he isn't planning to though, if I were you I'd have a quiet word pronto.'

'Easier said than done,' Sophie argued, 'I'm so busy prepping classes I haven't any time left to speak to him!'

'Linda's right though,' Andy chipped in.

'I know,' Sophie agreed. 'I know. So, how are things going?' she asked gingerly as Paul returned.

'We're ok aren't we love,' Paul answered, taking a seat in the last armchair. 'Tired. Alex doesn't get off to sleep until late and then he wakes again for a feed every two to three hours. It'll be worse when I go back to work but we'll figure something out.'

'How long do you have off work?' Andy asked

'Only a couple of weeks,' Paul groaned 'I wish it were longer.' He looked at Linda affectionately.

'If you need anything just call me,' Sophie told Linda sternly. 'I mean it, any time.' Sophie watched Linda wipe away another tear.

'Thanks hun,' she mumbled.

The roads were unusually busy as Andy drove them back to Sophie's house.

'You know when I went into the kitchen to help Paul wash up the cups he said he would be glad to get back to work for a rest!' Sophie laughed. 'Poor Paul, I bet Linda has him doing more than his fair share, she really is a sport that one.'

'Um, I'm not surprised,' Andy grinned. 'Still, they look happy beneath it all,' he said. 'Must be hard work. Anyway, listen,' his voice took on a gaggle of excitement. 'I've got a surprise for you,' he said as they rounded the corner into Convent Avenue. She looked up at him. 'I've had Bill go round today to complete the garden. Not the pond,' he stressed. 'I wasn't sure if you still wanted it.' He shifted into third gear as they gathered speed. 'Just tidy up and plant a few flowers around the borders. I thought it would be nicer for you, you know, after everything.' He beamed across at her as he slowed the van and parked in front of her driveway, where her little car sat peacefully.

'That's really sweet,' she murmured, her eyes sparkling. 'Thank you'

'Shall we?'

Sophie opened the van door to bounce out the van, virtually on the ground as Andy came to her side.

'You're getting good at that,' he laughed. 'Come on.'

She opened the front door and trod on the post, her heart felt heavy as she spotted the envelope poking out from the toe of her shoe. Another one. Frozen to the spot she gasped.

'What?' Andy came up behind her, kissed her neck and mockingly tried to budge her from the doormat.

'It's...' the words were caught in her throat. She felt numb.

'Come on woman, let's get inside,' Andy chuckled. 'What's wrong now?'

'It's…'

Andy glanced down at the doormat.

'Oh right. Sorry. Here, get inside and I'll ring the station,' he offered.

SO, YOU'VE FOUND THE TRUTH THEN…TAKE MY ADVICE, KEEP IT TO YOURSELF. IF YOU TAKE IT TO THE POLICE I WILL HAVE NO OPTION BUT TO SILENCE YOU. I MEAN IT, THE TRUTH HAS BEEN HAPPILY QUIET FOR YEARS, NO GOOD CAN COME OF IT NOW. FORGET ALL ABOUT IT. BURN THE LETTERS. I WARN YOU DO NOT MESS WITH ME OR I WILL HAVE TO KILL YOU. I AM NOT JOKING.

Chapter Sixteen

May 2009

Sophie put the receiver back into its cradle on the bedside table with a sigh of relief. The police had closed the case; the skeleton remains had been identified and would soon be released for burial. She had accepted Thomas Brody's remains as well; it would be a pity to separate them after all this time.

No news on the poison pen writer though, she shuddered at the thought. Whoever he was, he was still at large, and probably even more wound up now that she had disobeyed his wishes by taking the letters from the attic to the station. The police desk sergeant had assured her they were still working on identifying the writer, but she didn't hold out much hope. With no finger-prints or postmarks to go on there was precious little to help them. Even the last one, it being an actual death threat, shed no light on the situation. The station was apparently too under-manned to provide her with any protection. She looked across at Andy who slept soundlessly by her side. It had been a cheesy line she admitted with a smile, but in truth his presence did make her feel safer. She snuggled back down under the duvet and curled her body in line with his. Instinctively he wrapped her into his warmth and she lay, her eyes closed, contented. It was the weekend after all; she didn't need to get up just yet.

The sun streamed through the gap in the curtains and the birds twitted noisily. Sophie opened her eyes and glanced at the clock. Eleven had already dawned. She looked again in disbelief. No, she had been right, it was already eleven. As she untangled her body from Andy he began to stir. She couldn't remember the last time she had slept that late.

Andy moaned, reluctant to move.

'Sorry,' she whispered. 'It's late,' she explained as if that made any difference. He opened his eyes and cast her a lazy smile.

'Not much of a morning person,' he apologised. 'How late?'

'Eleven,' she said, hopping out of bed and reaching for her dressing gown. 'Do you want tea?'

'Yeah, I'll make it,' he offered finding some life in his legs as he swung them out of the bed.

The doorbell chimed tunelessly and they looked at each other dumbfounded.

'Expecting company?' she asked, heading for the window and peeking out. 'I think its Bill,' she was saying, leaning around the flimsy curtain. Andy slapped his forehead.

'Oh God, I'm sorry. I told him to come back this afternoon. I thought we'd still have the garden to do but it's virtually done isn't it, unless you've changed your mind about the pond?'

'Er, no, I don't think I want a pond after all. I'm not digging up any more of the lawn. God only knows what else is under there, well, it can stay there,' she told him stubbornly. 'You can send him away,' she smiled coyly. 'I'm not dressed to receive visitors,' she flashed her nightgown at him and giggled as she ran into the bathroom.

'Oh right,' he laughed, 'that's not fair. I have to go and talk to him now and all I can think about is…' he caught up with her, his arms around her waist and his chin on her shoulder. '…you,' he concluded. 'I'll see you in the shower,' he kissed her shoulder quickly, pulled on yesterday's jeans and top and made for the front door. 'Not too hot,' he called up the stairs.

She could hear him talking to Bill on the doorstep as she started the shower. The steam began to fill the room as she climbed in. Raised voices from downstairs pinpricked her hearing. Were they arguing?

192

Another shout; this time quite clearly 'get out of here!' it was Andy. She turned off the water and wrapped a towel around herself, opening the bathroom door to listen in. 'Put that thing away, for God's sake man, what's come over you?'

'I warned her,' Bill was yelling, 'where is she?' She could hear Andy breathing heavily, the hall telephone table went over with a crash. She opened the bathroom door and tip toed towards the stairs.

'What's going on?' she called.

'You bitch! I'm coming to kill you!' Bill was shouting his voice raspy and hoarse with the effort. She leapt back. Bill?

'Get back in the bedroom,' Andy shouted. 'Do it Soph. Call the police and lock the door!'

'Are you ok?' she called down the stairs. A flash of light caught her eye. Was that a knife? Were they wrestling in her hallway with a knife?

'Do it Soph, I mean it. NOW!!' Andy shouted. 'Bill, give it up, you're mad,' he struggled for breath as he attempted to pin Bill to the back of the front door, the knife blade dangerously gripped in Bill's fingers.

Sophie ran to the bedroom and dialled 999. Another crash downstairs and a short sharp cry. Her breath caught; was Andy ok?

'Which service please?'

'Yes, police please,' she tried to speak clearly but her breath was coming in sharp gasps and she couldn't control it. 'And an ambulance,' she demanded. 'Quickly, please hurry.'

'Glasgow connecting,' An electronic voice told her.

'Where are you?'

'26 Convent Avenue, Atwood,' she cried. 'Quickly.' Another crash downstairs. 'He's killing him, please hurry.'

'Emergency services are on their way. Stay on the line, what is your name?'

'Sophie Harris.'

'Ok Sophie, it's alright. Keep calm now. Tell me what's happening?'

'There's a mad man in my house; he's trying to kill my boyfriend, please hurry…I think he's got a knife…he wants to kill me,' she stammered.

'Ok, take a deep breath. Stay calm now. We're on our way to you. Where are you, exactly, are you in the house?'

'The bedroom, they're downstairs,' she was crying now, she hadn't noticed the tears staining her face until now. They fell hurriedly as she tried to breath normally but her vision was blurred with tears. She heard another yelp downstairs. Please don't let him be hurt, please don't let him be hurt…she dropped the receiver on the bed and ran to the door.

'Andy,' she cried, 'Andy!'

'I'm going to kill you, you bitch, I'm coming after you,' Bill's raspy voice shot up the stairs, ate up the space between them in an instant.

'Lock the door,' Andy shouted. 'Lock it Soph, do it now.'

'Andy! Are you ok?'

Something smashed below, the shattering tingling through the air like a siren.

'LOCK THE DOOR SOPH. I'm ok, get back in there,' his voice was heavy with the effort. She slammed it shut and ran back to the bed, picked up the phone.

'…Miss…Miss Harris.'

'I'm here,' she yelled into the phone. 'Hurry, please hurry.'

'Two minutes away,' the voice told her. 'Where exactly is the man with the knife?'

'They're right by the front door,' she whimpered. The tears were choking her. 'Andy is holding him back. Please hurry.'

'Can you lock the bedroom door?'

'No, I don't think so. The lock…it's broken…' She cried.

'What about the wardrobe, can you get in there?'

'Um…' Sophie started to drag the phone towards the wardrobe. 'Maybe,' she whispered. 'Ok…I can't close…the door,' she whimpered.

'Never mind Sophie. Tell me if they get closer to you. Do you know who the intruder is?'

'It's Bill!' she cried. 'I don't understand...I don't...understand why...'

'What is Bill's surname Sophie?'

Another yelp from downstairs made her flinch. Please let Andy be ok, please let Andy be ok, please...

'Sophie, are still with me, Sophie?' the operators voice was louder.

'I'm here,' she sobbed.

'What is Bill's surname Sophie?'

'I'm not sure,' she racked her mind frantically. Had Andy actually told her...no, he had never said...she had seen it though, on Andy's introduction letter...what did it say...Bill...it began with a J...

'Jason!' she yelled. 'I think its Jason.'

'Ok,' she heard frantic typing at the other end. 'You don't know why Bill Jason wants to harm you?'

'No! I haven't done anything...'

Sirens rang through her scrambled mind. She flinched and spun her head towards the window. Dragging the phone cord as far as possible she opened the curtains. Two police cars spun to a halt in front of her driveway, their black uniformed occupants sprang out as if on elastic.

'...Miss...Miss...Miss Harris...Sophie are you still there?'

'Yes, they're here,' she screamed. 'They're here...'

'Sophie, listen to me. Is the back door open?'

'No! Oh no, it's still locked,' she sobbed. 'I'll go...'

'No! Stay with me Miss...just stay on the line.' Sophie could hear crackling in the background, her own heart thumping, another smash downstairs and a tumble. 'Andy!' she screamed.

'Miss Harris?'

'Yes, hurry, I'm scared...'

'It's ok Sophie. Can you throw a key out the bedroom window to the police?'

'My key's are downstairs!' she screamed. 'I can't...I'll get them...'

'NO. Sophie, stay where you are. The police will break down your back door. You'll hear them gaining entry in two minutes. Stay on the line now Sophie, listen to me. It's going to be ok.'

Another siren died outside. The ambulance.

'Sophie, we are proceeding with caution. An AVR unit is on its way, just breath deeply now. Stay calm.'

A loud smash made her jump.

'Hurry!' she screamed. 'Andy!' she called.

There was no answer.

'Andy!' she cried into a sob.

Another smash vibrated through the house like an earthquake.

'Sophie, it's ok, the AVR unit has arrived and the police are gaining entry now. Stay on the line Miss Harris.'

'Ok,' she mouthed, blinded by tears. Andy...he hadn't answered... please let him be ok, please let him be ok...

With one fatal hammer the back door was down. She heard loud voices and scuffles. A struggle, a sigh, more voices. The clink of metal...

'Right ok, Sophie, the police have made an arrest. You can go downstairs now. The officer will speak to you.'

'Thank you,' she cried, tossed the phone on the bed behind her and made for the door, the towel still wrapped around her wet glistening body like a shield.

'Sophie?' it was Andy's voice. The relief swept over her like a wave. She almost fell down the stairs. Where was he...why couldn't she see him? Was it her imagination...

'I'll get you,' Bill was shouting as the officer dragged him over the back door that now lay on the kitchen floor. 'I'll get you.' Bill's face was unrecognisable, twisted into a picture of hatred. A cold shiver pulsated through her. The police constable whipped him away out the door from sight. She shivered again.

Then she spotted him.

'Andy!' she fell from one step to another until he caught her at the bottom, wrapping his arms around her tightly. They clung to each other, the desperation and relief mingled into strength. 'My hero,' she whispered. He smiled at her.

'It was nothing,' he half laughed, his fingers toying with her loose wet hair.

'Are you ok?' her voice a shade above a whisper.

'I'm fine,' he assured. 'I'm fine.' She ran her fingertips lightly over a cut on his eyebrow.

'Miss Harris?' An officer stood hovering by their side, breaking into their little spell. 'I'm sorry Miss Harris, but we need to ask you a few questions. And Sir, I'll need you to go to the hospital. Just routine.'

'Yes of course,' Andy said.

'Can I just...' Sophie indicated the towel and the officer nodded. 'I'm coming with you,' she called to Andy as she sprinted up the stairs. 'Don't go without me,' she called as she darted up the stairs.

The adrenaline pumped through her like a current but she felt weak as she sank into a skirt and comfortable shoes. She pulled a light top over her head and ran a brush quickly through her mated hair.

'Miss Harris,' the officer began as she reached the bottom step. 'We'll send someone around to see to the door,' he promised. She gave it a short glance and nodded. 'Do you know the intruder?'

'Not really, no...'

'He's my employee,' Andy ventured. 'Part-time. I can't believe he'd do this.'

'Why do you think he came here to attack you Miss Harris?'

'I've no idea,' she shrugged her shoulders, still quivering from the shock.

'And Sir, do you have any idea why he would wish Miss Harris harm?'

'No, none at all officer, I can't believe it,' Andy reached for her hand, the look of confusion spread over his face. 'I just can't understand it.'

'Ok, ok' the officer flipped his notebook closed. 'We'll let you know the outcome' he said. 'In the meantime, I want you to make your way to the ambulance outside. I'll leave an officer here until you return. Hopefully we'll have the door back in place by then'

'Officer?'

'Yes Miss?'

'Do you think he was the one writing the letters?'

'Well it's too early to say but we'll certainly be interviewing him about that Miss, don't you worry.'

Sophie nodded, 'thanks,' she said. Andy took her hand and led her towards the ambulance. Most of the streets' occupants were standing at their gates, a huddle had gathered as close as the police would allow and the road was blocked with police cars, letting only the ambulance any movement.

Sophie looked blankly at her neighbours, whom she had barely gotten to know, wondered briefly if they would ever remember anything else about her other than the tragic scene they found themselves witnessing today. One thing was certain she thought; they would all be round wanting to be friends simply to find out what had happened. Perhaps it was this way too for Elise, or rather for Frederick after Elise's death...

As they climbed in the back of the ambulance Bill was being pushed forcefully into the back of the police squad car, his face a picture of contorted rage. Andy pushed Sophie towards the ambulance so she wouldn't see him.

'Why does he hate me so much?'

'I don't know sweetheart,' Andy answered honestly. 'I've no idea. Try not to think about it,' he advised, his fingers stroking the back of her hand. The ambulance left Convent Avenue quietly, much quieter than when it had arrived.

The air was still and warm, the sun brightly shining through the clouds like a kaleidoscope. Only a small gathering had turned out to pay their respects to Elise and Thomas. Amongst them Sophie stood, her hands knotted together in the black lacy gloves. Andy stood solemnly by her side. She had never seen him in a suit before; he looked dashing. Behind her were her parents, her mother unable to resist the odd floral accessory in the form of a silk scarf.

Although she had extended the invitation to the descendents of Thomas's family she was secretly pleased they hadn't arrived. It seemed fitting they should concentrate on their current day problems and deep down she didn't know how she was supposed to react. What did one do when faced with such clumsy behaviour?

The vicar looked like a domino in his black and white outfit. He was reading from the bible, a verse Sophie had heard many times before. She found herself looking at the small coffin that housed both her great-great Aunt Elise and her lover, Thomas Brody.

The vicar, surprisingly, had agreed to bury Elise and Tom together. Adultery was a sin in the eyes of the church, yet she had been glad when he had agreed that it made little matter now, their remains having been laid side by side for so many years already. After all, Frederick himself had put them together back in 1935, so he could hardly object even if he were able to. Nearby, the grave of her great-great uncle Frederick stood next to his parents. Sophie wondered what he would have made of it all. If his letter had been anything to go by he may have started out life as a poor example for a man but sadly it had taken the death of his wife to turn his character around. If only he had been more affectionate before, perhaps the lives of Elise and Thomas would have been saved. Or maybe not...Elise and Thomas had loved each other. Maybe their fate was sealed from the day they met... who could say.

The vicar was nearing the end of his lesson and the pallbearers began to lower the coffin into the ground. She reached for Andy's hand and found he had been hovering, in anticipation for her. After such a short acquaintance he seemed to know just when she would need him, even before she knew it herself.

Sophie picked up the rose she had bought, fingered the petals fleetingly and let it float down to the coffin.

'Hello, it's nice to meet you,' Sophie's mother patted the pink floral seat by her side. Andy sat as instructed. 'I'm so glad you were there, when I think what could have happened to my dear Sophie…'

'I'm fine mum, I promise,' Sophie urged. 'Today went well didn't it,' she attempted but her mother was having none of it.

'Oh dear, that wretched man, I hope they throw the book at him!' she spluttered. 'I mean, how awful, brandishing a knife about like that, on a Sunday too!' she complained.

The sun shot through the room like a flame and Sophie blinked against it. Her father adjusted the curtains but her mother was not put off her flow.

'I don't think that mad men have Sunday's off Mrs Harris,' Andy soothed. 'But Sophie is fine now,' he assured her.

'Thanks only to you my dear boy,' she stroked his head as if he were a puppy. 'We are eternally grateful to you, and you can call me Ethel dear.'

'Yes son,' her father chipped in curtly. 'Thank you,' he looked towards his wife. 'That's enough my dear,' he soothed, 'you'll embarrass the poor lad. Shall we have some tea?'

Her father had already changed back into his brown corduroy trousers and bore a blue knitted jumper over his shirt, the peek of his red tie just bursting out the top. He stood proudly by the mantelpiece. Sophie wondered if he had copied the stance from an old black and white movie picture.

'Thanks Dad,' Sophie said as her mother jostled out the room into the kitchen. Her father gave her a knowing smile. 'You're her hero now,' Sophie smiled at Andy. 'You'll be forgiven all manor of sins I expect, and probably be told to keep me in line too,' she laughed. Her father smiled.

'She means well but she's a bit of a scatter brain, you'll get used to her my boy. Blimey, I'm starving, where's the cake? She's been out there baking most of yesterday and again this morning,' he spluttered 'you'd think there'd be too much for her to carry…'

'I'd better see if she needs a hand,' Sophie rose from the armchair but before she had made it two steps the mass of badly shaped floral dress, that was her mother, returned with a clatter of cups and saucers on a hostess trolley.

'Tea and cake,' I think she chirped joyfully. 'Andy my dear, won't you have a slice, I made it myself you know…'

'Wherever did you get that, woman?' her father demanded

'It was in the jumble sale at the church hall last week; you remember, you were with me. Old Mrs Betts from across the road dropped it in for me last Thursday,' she declared, then turning towards Andy 'his memory isn't what it used to be,' she chuckled. 'Nice sturdy thing I thought,' she justified, giving the trolley a bit of a wobble. 'Just the job for today,' she continued, the knife sinking easily into the sponge cake.

The tea and cake was indeed delicious. Despite having issued invitations to those who had bothered to attend the service no-one had been forthcoming so the wake was a simple affair, just the four of them in her parent's living room.

'Did you know any of the others at the funeral?' Sophie asked her father. He shook his head at her as he bit into the last chunk of carrot cake on his plate.

'I expect they were just poor old souls with nowhere better to be,' her mother commented.

'Nosy neighbours more like,' Andy announced. 'I recognised quite a few from your street,' he told Sophie. 'They were gawping at us too, the other day,' he smiled. The sun had cast a shadow across half his face and she realised again how very handsome he was.

'See, like I said,' her mother nodded cheerfully. 'Poor souls with nothing better to do,' she nodded in affirmation and sipped her tea.

'Just as well the Brody family didn't come anyway,' her father said, 'or whatever their name is now.'

'Jason,' Andy filled in. 'Bill Jason; he was such a nice guy, I still can't believe he'd do a thing like this.'

'Why did he?' her father wanted to know.

'The police said he was Cheryl's son; it was Cheryl who murdered Elise and Tom,' Sophie explained and sipped her tea. 'Cheryl married again when she was 48 and had Bill.'

'Bit late in life wasn't it,' her mother decided, 'to be having children I mean.'

'Yeah, was a bit,' Andy agreed

'Anyway,' Sophie continued 'she had Bill. Accordingly to Bill she felt guilty about the killings and started keeping a journal in which she confessed. She went to church daily until she was too weak to walk there. Bill kept the journal after she died. He never told anyone about his mother's crime and didn't want it coming out now.'

'Shouldn't think he did,' her father sighed. 'Very sad, hint of madness in their blood line I'd say.'

'So that's why he wrote those horrible notes to you my love?' her mother queried

'Yes, he guessed from the newspapers that my garden was the one and he just didn't want his wife and daughters to know that his mother was the killer.'

'And the religious reading?' her father piped up. 'What was the meaning of that? He can't have been trying to protect you?'

'Inspector Allen reckons he was doing just that, in his muddle-headed way; trying to make us cover it all up and forget about it,' Sophie explained.

'Do you think he'll go to prison?' he asked.

'Don't know,' Sophie mused.

'Probably an institution for the mental health,' her father suggested.

'I suppose it's my fault really,' Andy said. Sophie shot him a look.

'Don't be daft, how can it be your fault? You were the one who saved me from him!'

'I employed him. I didn't check for madness when I took him on and I told him about the garden. I had to, before I could let him work on it, in case something else turned up.'

'Don't be silly my lad,' her fathers stern voice boomed. 'It ain't no more your fault than it is mine for not having the garden dug up when my own mother suspected years ago. Let's leave it now.' Sophie watched her father take a sip of his tea, took Andy's hand in hers and smiled at her mother. Her father had spoken, that was the end of the subject.

'So, Mum, Dad,' she began. 'We have some news for you.' She looked to Andy and he nodded.

'You tell them,' he smiled.

Sophie held up her left hand. An engagement ring adorned her finger. Her mother nearly fainted with delight.

23rd May 2009   Issue No 3079
ATWOOD CHRONICLE

Murder Mysteries Solved!

The mystery behind the disappearance to two local residents in 1935 has finally been resolved. Elise Harris and Thomas Brody were discovered buried beneath the rear gardens of Elise's former home in Covent Avenue.

The remains were, quite literally, dug up by the new owner of the property, Elise's descendent Sophie Harris and her fiancé, Andrew Taylor. 'We were just starting to dig for a new pond,' said Andrew. 'There was lots of renovation work to be done and we thought we would make a start whilst the weather was good.' Neither party expected to discover the bones of the long lost relative Elise who was said to have moved away from the area and died some years previously, despite no death certificate ever having been created.

Cheryl Brody, now deceased, is accused of committing the deed although Frederick Harris, also deceased, is said to be guilty of burying the bodies once he had discovered them in his living room, and without informing the police. The chosen burial place was a prime location for a pond, near a patio that hadn't always been part of the garden. Stereotype, I hear you, but I kid you not, this is the actual truth. Perhaps when faced with bodies to bury most of us would automatically build a patio as well. Who knows what the mind will command of you until the time demands you to test it out?

Theories are being investigated that Frederick Harris wanted the bodies to be found after his death, and perhaps this determined the path his inheritance took. We may never know but one thing is for sure, Cheryl Brody, had she lived, would be going behind bars and not a day too soon.

A local man, descendant of Cheryl, has been accused of sending threatening letters to Sophie Harris.

'My client is not crazy,' claims the defendant's solicitor Rebecca Barnes of Knightsbridge Law Firm. 'He was distraught at the thought of the truth coming out and his family's reputation being ruined. Any actions he may have taken would have been whilst the balance of his mind was disturbed.' A bold statement indeed. The trial is set to take place in December of this year at Ipswich Crown Court. We'll keep you abreast of the details as and when we have them.